Still can't get en

Popular Mills & Boon® Blaze® author
Debbi Rawlins keeps readers in the saddle
with her continuing miniseries

MADE IN MONTANA

Since the McAllisters opened a dude ranch catering
sleepy town of Blackfoot Falls
lot more interesting…

ls on a hot cowboy with

' BLUE JEAN NIGHT

I THE NIGHT

/ CHRISTMAS NIGHT

STILL THE ONE

NEEDS TO KNOW
June 2013

HIS MOMENT ON
ugust 2013

d remember,
ys are Made in Montana!

Dear Reader,

One of the great joys of writing a series with recurring
characters is the anticipation factor. For me, I mean.
Ever since I wrote the first character sketch of Wallace
Gunderson, that horrible man who appeared in the first
book, I knew he would bring a lot of secrets and lies
along with him. Enough to rock Blackfoot Falls down
to the roots.

But, he also brought along troubled, angry Matt
Gunderson, his son. Matt had run the moment he
was able and became a bull-riding champion. Now he's
come back, and no one is more shocked than Rachel
McAllister, who never got over the love of her life.

It's not exactly a modern version of *Romeo and Juliet,*
but it was even more fun to write than I'd imagined.
I hope you like it, too.

All my best,

Debbi Rawlins

YOU'RE STILL THE ONE

BY
DEBBI RAWLINS

First published in Great Britain 2013
by Mills & Boon, an imprint of Harlequin (UK) Limited,
Eton House, 18-24 Paradise Road, Richmond, Surrey TW9 1SR

© Debbi Quattrone 2013

ISBN: 978 0 263 90507 6

30-0413

Harlequin (UK) policy is to use papers that are natural, renewable and recyclable products and made from wood grown in sustainable forests. The logging and manufacturing processes conform to the legal environmental regulations of the country of origin.

Printed and bound in Spain
by Blackprint CPI, Barcelona

Debbi Rawlins lives in central Utah, out in the country, surrounded by woods and deer and wild turkeys. It's quite a change for a city girl who didn't even know where the state of Utah was until a few years ago. Of course, unfamiliarity has never stopped her. Between her junior and senior years of college, she spontaneously left her home in Hawaii and bummed around Europe for five weeks by herself. And much to her parents' delight, returned home with only a quarter in her wallet.

1

WITHOUT FEELING AN OUNCE of guilt, Rachel McAllister, still wearing her blue flannel pajamas and comfy robe, left her mother in the kitchen to make breakfast and plopped down on the leather couch in the den with her laptop. Today was her birthday and she was taking the day off. Well, not the whole day. That would be impossible unless she left the Sundance. Upstairs in the guest wing, a dozen women were in the midst of waking up, applying war paint or debating over which inappropriate outfit to wear for their sleigh ride through the foothills.

This was February in Montana, the temperature near freezing and no strongly worded advice Rachel posted on the Sundance's website made a bit of difference. The women came dressed more to impress her brothers than to stay warm. God bless the McAllister boys. All three of them were terrific ranchers, even better eye candy, and the reservations by adventurous single women kept on coming. Good for the bottom line each month, not so good for Rachel's sad little life.

She couldn't complain, though, since it had been her idea to make part of the family homestead a dude ranch. They needed the income until their real business of raising cattle, and the economy in general, recovered. Then she'd be free again. Free to pursue a career, live in the bright lights of the city, wear high heels and orange sweaters that clashed horribly with her auburn hair, without anyone giving her a second look. And hopefully, barter her master's degree for a cool job with a hotel chain that would send her to even cooler places.

But the ranch—her family—had paid for that graduate degree and she owed them big-time. They didn't feel that way, of course. She was the youngest, the only girl, and her mother and brothers would do anything for her—including keeping her in the dark about the family's floundering finances while paying her tuition. Yet she should've known…would have seen it if she hadn't been so self-absorbed and living the good life in Dallas.

Through five generations of McAllisters the three-thousand-acre Sundance had been one of the most prosperous ranches around. Not once had it occurred to her that they were struggling just like any other business in the livestock industry that was dependent on beef consumption and gas prices.

No, she'd turned a blind eye for years, going to school, cashing the monthly expense checks they sent her…. The idea shamed her so much she couldn't bear to think about it. And she wouldn't. Not today. Not on her twenty-sixth birthday. She'd cut herself a break. Just for a few hours…

Her laptop stirred to life and she checked email first, grinning at the string of funny birthday messages from her college friends. Her sophomore roommate, Ashley, had sent an e-card of a male stripper strategically holding a birthday cake. Rachel laughed, glancing toward the door to make sure she was still alone.

She opened several more e-cards and found that everyone seemed to be on the same cheesy track. The semi-naked men would be far more amusing if she hadn't been celibate for so damn long. Almost eight months since she'd returned home, and before that another four since she'd split from her casual relationship with Tom, a third-year law student. Great. Her dry spell was about to reach the anniversary mark.

Sighing, she clicked the mouse on last year's birthday bash. Twenty-five, a milestone according to her friends who'd used the excuse to go all out. She smiled at the picture of Katy popping the cork. It had been eight-thirty, and they hadn't even made it to their first club yet.

"Ah, here you are."

At the sound of Jamie's voice, Rachel nearly lost her laptop. She kept it from sliding to the floor but didn't close it in time.

Jamie leaned over to better see the picture. "Oh, my God, is that you?"

"Um, yep." Rachel set the laptop to the side and closed it. "What's up?"

"Let me see." With an elbow, Jamie nudged her over, then dropped to the couch beside her. "When was that taken?"

Rachel really liked her brother Cole's girlfriend and was thrilled she'd moved to the Sundance just last week. They'd become fast friends even before the move, while Jamie had been a guest. But Rachel wasn't sure she wanted to share this other side of herself yet. Her family didn't know about her wanting to leave and they'd be hurt. "It's pretty boring stuff since you don't know anyone."

"I know you. Happy birthday, by the way. That's why I came looking for you."

"Thanks. I think." Rachel put her hands on her cheeks and tested the elasticity of her skin.

"Oh, please." Jamie snorted. "Now you're just gonna piss me off. Wait till *you're* twenty minutes away from the big three-0."

"You have two years yet."

"It goes by fast." Jamie's gaze went to the laptop. "Were those Halloween pictures?"

"Hey." Rachel made a face. "They're from my last birthday."

"You're joking." Jamie stared at her. "Come on, let me see."

Rachel got it. All she wore were jeans and oversize flannel

shirts these days. Perfect for the ranch. "All right, look, you can't say anything to Cole, or anyone else."

Jamie shrugged, obviously confused. "Okay."

Rachel opened the laptop and brought up the pictures, surrendering the computer when Jamie reached for it.

"You were still in Dallas last year, right?" Jamie studied the image of Rachel in a snug pink top, short black leather skirt and glittery charcoal-colored stilettos. She was wearing full makeup, her fuchsia lips puckered in a kiss she was blowing to the camera. The same pink color as her top wove through her bangs.

She nodded, even though Jamie was too absorbed with the radical image to look up. "I was working on my master's and sharing a house with three other women."

Jamie clicked on the picture of Chloe, Katy and Liz, who all looked effortlessly big-city chic. "Your roommates?"

"We met while living in the dorms, then found a house we could afford right before senior year. My share didn't cost any more than a dorm room." Only when Jamie gave her a curious look did Rachel realize she'd sounded defensive.

"They threw you the party, I assume."

"Um, no party. We were getting ready to go club hopping when someone snapped these. The fun started much later."

Jamie grinned at the champagne toast they were making in the next photo. "Please tell me you didn't get hammered too early."

"Why do you think we had to chronicle the night?"

Jamie laughed. "Seriously?"

"No." Rachel smiled. "I was fine. If nothing else, those ridiculous heels kept me in line."

"You mean those weren't part of your normal attire?"

"More than you might think. I have three other pairs."

"You wild woman." Jamie eyed her with amusement. "You know you've totally destroyed my image of you, right?"

Rachel sighed. "Absolutely."

Jamie angled the laptop toward her. "Cute. Who's this?"

She glanced at the photo. "Tom. We hung out for almost a year, when we weren't too busy." He was ambitious, so was she, and they'd been good together until they weren't. Neither of them had had a problem with saying adios when their schedules got too crazy.

"So you guys still keep in touch, or is it over?"

"Both. He wrote me when he passed his bar exam, and then when he moved to join a law firm in Denver." Rachel paused. Explaining too much was tricky. No telling what Cole had revealed about the Sundance's beleaguered financial situation. "We knew that eventually we'd each go where our careers took us."

Jamie frowned a little, half closed the laptop and studied Rachel's face. "You weren't planning on staying here," she said, lowering her voice.

Rachel glanced over her shoulder. "Swear you won't repeat anything I tell you," she said, turning back to Jamie. "Not even to Cole."

"Of course I won't, but that doesn't mean you have to tell me anything. Really. I won't be offended." Jamie passed the laptop back to Rachel. "We all have secrets."

Sighing, she offered a smile. "I'm sorry. I know you wouldn't betray a confidence. That was just me being insecure."

"You? Insecure? Uh-uh. But I know, we all have those days." Jamie started to get up.

"Wait. This isn't some top secret thing, it's just that I don't know what Cole told you about why we opened for guests."

Jamie settled down again. "He mentioned the Sundance was struggling financially and that the dude ranch was your idea. Which was brilliant, by the way, but I also understand it's not easy for everyone in the family to accept."

"At this point, I think the guys have made peace with the

idea. Especially since they know it's a temporary solution and we've already seen a profit. But part of the deal was that I handle that side of the business."

"And you feel stuck."

Rachel gave a small shrug. "I wouldn't say I'm stuck, but it did alter my plans somewhat."

"Meaning?"

Rachel let out a rush of air. "I was only going to stay for part of the summer, spend time with my mom while I decided between two hotel chains that had tried to recruit me."

Jamie's eyebrows went up. "Um, I think that qualifies for more than somewhat. Wow. I don't know if you remember a conversation we had last August about you staying at the Sundance, but I figured something was off."

"I remember." The conversation had been about whether Rachel could be happy staying home. "I'm not looking for sympathy. This is exactly where I'm supposed to be, doing exactly what I'm meant to be doing. I owe my family. If I have to stay here another five years then—"

"Oh, God…you and Cole and your hyper sense of responsibility…." Jamie's lips twitched in a wry smile. "Must run in the family."

"You don't understand. Cole paid my tuition every semester, then agreed to graduate school, even though the ranch was in trouble."

"And yet the Sundance is still here. There's food on the table every night." Jamie touched her arm. "You think he would do one thing differently?"

"I don't know. No."

"Do you think Cole or the rest of your family would want you to sacrifice your future for the sake of the ranch, or for them?"

Boy, was this turning out to be a shitty birthday. Rachel

rubbed her eyes. "I know it's hard for you to understand, Jamie."

"Because I don't have siblings? Or because my parents were more concerned with serving their country than raising me?"

Rachel gasped. "I didn't mean it like that." What was wrong with her? She knew Jamie's background and of course she would jump to that conclusion. "I swear I didn't—"

"Relax. Even if that's what you were getting at, you'd have a point." She waved dismissively. "It's just that I'm pretty sure your family never thought you went to college so you could open a dude ranch."

Rachel smiled. "I promise you my brothers haven't given it that much thought."

"Hmm, yeah…okay." Jamie let out a short laugh. "I'll give you that one. But your mom?"

Rachel slumped against the back of the couch. "I've spent a few sleepless nights worrying about that. Tiring as it is, she loves having guests to look after and chat with, and she's probably hoping this will be enough for me to stay." She sighed. "I'm really glad you're here, and when Shea makes the move it'll be even better, but I need new scenery. I need a challenge."

The expression on Jamie's face made Rachel feel worse, and a little defensive again. Clearly she also wanted Rachel to stay. But Jamie couldn't fully understand. Her situation was different. She was a travel blogger. Sure she'd moved her home base here but she'd be on the road to faraway exotic locales half the time. Besides, living on a ranch was still novel for her. Just as it would be for Jesse's girlfriend, Shea, once she arrived. For Rachel it was same old, same old…. Even so, it would be a hell of a long time before leaving was possible.

Jamie's thoughtful gaze moved to the laptop. Then back to Rachel. "Wanna go to Tahiti?"

Rachel laughed. "What on earth are you talking about?"

"You should share travel duties with me," she said, "while I fill in here for you. It would give me a break. You, too."

"That's crazy." Rachel wouldn't admit it, but the idea sent her pulse skittering.

"I'm serious. Think about it, and we'll talk more later. Tonight your mom has a special dinner planned, with cake afterward. You know all about it…." she said, and Rachel nodded. "But today it's you and me, kiddo. We're hitting town, going to The Cut and Curl."

Laughing, Rachel wondered if Jamie had ever set foot in Blackfoot Falls's only beauty parlor. Not hair salon, that would be overreaching.

"Wait." Jamie held up a hand. "We're going to have the works—manicure, pedicure, coiffing…and streaks. How about purple this year?"

"You're crazy," Rachel said, shaking her head. "Have you ever been to The Cut and Curl?"

"No." She grinned. "And this is the best part—after, we'll go to the Watering Hole for shots and beer. Who knows? There may be someone new in town and you'll get laid."

"Keep it down," Rachel said, when Jamie's voice rose with her enthusiasm.

Jamie clamped a hand over her mouth, and giggling like schoolgirls, they both swung glances toward the door.

"Come on," Jamie said, gesturing excitedly. "Get up. Get ready while I help your mom and Hilda with breakfast."

It was seven-thirty. Marge's Diner and the hardware store were the only things open in Blackfoot Falls. But Rachel didn't care. She was feeling much better. She grabbed her laptop and ran upstairs. Maybe today would end up being special after all.

"DEAR GOD, I HOPE THOSE things aren't alive." Jamie stood with her hand on the doorknob, staring at the trio of wigs on foam mannequin heads in The Cut and Curl window display.

Rachel bumped her from behind to get her moving. "Keep it up and you'll be the topic of conversation at every dinner table tonight."

"Please." Jamie snorted. "That was so last week when I arrived with the moving truck."

"Do not underestimate these women," Rachel whispered, and pushed harder.

Jamie was forced to either open the door or smash her nose against the glass. Still it didn't stop her from glancing over her shoulder and murmuring, "You know they're all dissecting me five ways to Sunday, worried I'm not good enough for Cole."

She wouldn't argue that one. People around here were proprietary about their hometown boys as a rule, but the McAllister brothers, Cole in particular, were the cream that rose to the top.

They both stepped inside, a slight whiff of perm solution making Rachel consider turning around. Naturally, Sally, the owner, and her cousin Roxy—the only other beautician in the shop—had already spotted them outside. So had the two customers sitting under the dryers, one of them being Ruth Wilson, a popular teacher now retired. Rachel almost didn't recognize Mrs. Perkins until she poked her head out from under the noisy plastic bubble.

"Happy birthday, Rachel," she said. "I ran into your mama at the Food Mart buying ingredients for your cake yesterday."

"Thank you, Mrs. Perkins." No such thing as a surprise party in Blackfoot Falls. If anyone ever pulled off such a feat, it would be one for the record books.

Looking pleased that she'd been the first to acknowledge Rachel's birthday, Libby Perkins waited for everyone else to follow suit, then ducked back under the dryer.

Jamie was trying to control a smile and not gawk at the dated magazine cutouts on the pink walls as she stepped up to the counter where Sally leaned a plump hip.

Rachel remembered something. "Do not ask for a pedicure," she told Jamie low enough not to be overheard.

Sally stopped blowing on her red glossy nails. "What can I do for you young ladies?"

Jamie hesitated, then frowned at Rachel. "Seriously?"

"Trust me."

Sally's fake brows lifted in question. They'd been plucked clean and penciled back in to match her big blond hair. The 'do was really something. Each year she seemed to tease the crown a bit higher—probably her version of a facelift—and poor Jamie, since laying eyes on her up close, seemed to be having trouble breaking contact.

Rachel bit back a grin. "I'd like a shampoo and blow-out, a manicure, too, if you have time."

"Sure, we do." Sally gave Jamie the once-over. "What about your friend?"

"Same for me." Jamie smiled, and subtly nudged Rachel. "And streaks. Just one for me, blue if you have it. Rachel?"

Sally straightened, a twinkle lighting her eyes. "You want a streak in your hair, Rachel?"

"Oh, why not? What color choices do you have? Purple would be good."

Roxy moved in next to Sally, her eyes wide under her mousy brown bangs. "Your mama's gonna have a cow."

"Guess what?" Rachel leaned over the counter. Excitement shining in their faces, anxious for any tidbit, both women met her halfway. "I'm twenty-six years old."

Sally drew back with a humph. "You saying you don't listen to your mama anymore?"

"Nope." Rachel smiled. "I'm saying she hasn't told me what to do in a long time."

Clearly disappointed, Roxy shuffled back to her workstation. Anyone who knew her could pick out which spot was hers by the Elvis photos outlining the wall mirror. He'd passed away before she was born, but she'd been in love with him since the eighth grade.

"Give me a minute to get ready for you." Sally hustled toward the back station with the turquoise shampoo bowl.

Rachel knew the wait would be a bit longer so Sally's nails could dry. She turned her back on the shop so only Jamie could hear her. "The place looks old-fashioned but Sally isn't a bad stylist. She keeps up on trends. Even tried jazzing up the place to keep the younger women from going to Kalispell for their haircuts, but the older clientele complained."

"Where do you get yours cut?"

Rachel smiled wryly. "Kalispell."

"Okay, next time you go…"

"Yep, I'll let you know."

Jamie picked up a hairstyle magazine left on the counter and flipped through it. "So what's the deal about not asking for a pedicure?"

"I doubt Sally is set up for it. Around here goats and horses have their hooves trimmed, and women cut their own toenails."

"This is sad. I don't know when you're kidding anymore."

"Sometimes it's an adjustment for me, too. I lived in Dallas for over six years, remember."

Jamie sighed. "Then I guess I shouldn't ask for a Brazilian either."

Rachel laughed loudly enough that Sally and Roxy both sent her curious looks. Sally waved them back to her station, and before Rachel took the lead, she murmured to Jamie, "I dare you."

"I'm not worried. They'll be too busy talking about you and your purple streak, Miss Goody Two-Shoes."

"Oh, they'll be whispering all right…about what a horrible influence you are on me."

This time Jamie burst out laughing. "I'm screwed either way."

Sally motioned for Rachel to sit in her chair. "You ladies are in mighty fine moods. You just wait till you're looking down the barrel of *forty*-six and see how chipper you are." She shook out a plastic pink cape and draped it over Rachel.

"What would you know about that?" Rachel lifted her hair so Sally could tie the strings. "You can't be a day over thirty yourself."

Sally chuckled. She'd been telling people she was thirty-nine for so long, her age had remained a true mystery. But forty-six sounded about right.

Rolling her eyes, Jamie sank onto Roxy's chair and was sheathed with her own plastic cape.

"You two serious about putting in streaks?" Sally asked.

In unison they assured her they were, and she eagerly pulled out color samples. Roxy didn't seem as impressed, and she gladly stood by while Sally mixed the two selected shades.

Mrs. Perkins's dryer went off and she started to say something when the door opened. All heads turned toward Louise. Her cheeks red, she looked as if she'd run all the way from her fabric store, a pair of scissors in one hand, and a silver thimble on her right thumb.

"You're not gonna believe who I just saw going into Abe's Variety." Her gaze panned the room, her eyes bright and excited.

"Well, go ahead, tell us before you have a stroke," Sally said impatiently.

Searching each face until she was satisfied she had everyone's full attention, Louise took another dramatic pause, then deliberately met Rachel's eyes and said, "Matt Gunderson."

2

RACHEL FELT THE BLOOD drain from her face. She didn't think she'd said anything out loud or made a weird noise, but she might have. All the other women were staring at her, including Jamie.

For pity's sake, Rachel hadn't seen him in ten years. Yeah, she'd had a thing for him once, but she'd been a kid, only sixteen when he left town. The few people who'd suspected her crush hadn't taken it seriously. For two reasons—he was three years older than her, already a man, and he was a Gunderson. Everyone in Blackfoot Falls knew McAllisters and Gundersons didn't mix. Not if Matt's father had anything to do with it, anyway.

"Matt Gunderson," Sally repeated with a soft murmur. "He was a damn fine-looking young man last I saw him. Tall and lean, with those bedroom blue eyes… Got his pa's looks. Wallace was real handsome in his twenties and thirties, before he started drinking heavy. What's it been, ten years since Matt left?"

"Good thing he didn't end up with Wallace's nasty disposition." Louise said. "Of course a decade is a long time…anything could've happened. I suppose he might be just as rotten as his father by now."

"Not Matt," Ruth Wilson said, the adamant shake of her head brooking no argument. "He was a quiet, sweet boy, and very smart, too." He'd been her student, just like everyone under age forty living in Salina County had been at one time or another. "I'd hoped Matthew would go to college. I certainly encouraged him to give it a try. So did his mama. By the way, he was here for her funeral three years ago. Seems you ladies have forgotten."

"I didn't forget." Libby Perkins sniffed. "Catherine Gunderson was a lovely woman. I don't know a soul who didn't attend her funeral. The way I hear it, Matt came back two weeks before she died, stayed glued to her bedside, saw to her burial arrangements the day she passed, then left an hour after the services."

Rachel hadn't gone to the funeral. She'd been in Dallas, studying for finals, and hadn't learned of Mrs. Gunderson's passing until a week later. By delaying the news, her mother had saved her from making the decision to return for the services. Selfishly, Rachel hadn't minded. The timing had been bad as far as school went, and she hadn't wanted to see Matt under such sad circumstances.

The women continued talking about the Gundersons, mostly Wallace and his haggard appearance of late. They speculated on whether it was due to drinking or if his failing health was the reason Matt had suddenly shown up. Though it was no secret the two had been estranged the minute Matt left a decade ago.

Rachel quit listening and tried to think about something else. Except it was difficult to ignore the jittery feeling in her stomach. She couldn't even distract herself by talking to Jamie, not without the others hearing them. But the way Jamie kept shooting her inquisitive glances, it was obvious what was on her mind. The trouble was, Rachel hadn't decided how much she wanted to share about Matt.

It was ridiculous that she was having any reaction at all. Absurd to be replaying scenes of hot summer afternoons they'd spent swimming in Mill Creek after she'd lured him away from his chores. She'd been a kid, not even a junior yet, and incensed that his father was so mean and making Matt work all the time.

She'd pretended to be hiking that first day she followed him to the fence line that separated their properties. And he'd pretended to believe her. After that it got to be a regular Friday thing throughout the rest of the summer. She'd just show up at the section of fence he was mending. For several weeks he only smiled at her teasing and flirting. Then one day he'd yanked off his hat and unbuttoned his shirt, and she'd nearly peed her pants.

The sneak had worn swim trunks under his jeans, but he'd let her go through her usual song and dance trying to tempt him. They'd raced each other to the creek. He'd let her win, then gave her a victory kiss. It was brief, nothing hot or steamy, but at the time she'd been convinced she was having a heart attack.

Until then, she'd never kissed a boy, at least not a real kiss, and she'd wanted more. But he'd slammed on the brakes, kept her at arm's length. He'd said she was too young…anything beyond kissing wasn't going to happen. It hadn't stopped her from lying in the tall grass after he returned to work, staring up at the clear blue sky, daydreaming, debating whether she'd be a modern woman and keep her last name or become Rachel Gunderson.

To her annoyance, Matt had kept his word all summer, clear through fall, up to her sixteenth birthday. The kisses had grown more frustrating and sometimes he'd rubbed against her breasts, but always through her shirt. By February, a day before her birthday, she'd made up her mind. Half the girls in her class had boasted of having sex, and she decided she would lose her virginity to Matt that night when they met behind the calving shed. She'd taken a blanket with her, confident she could entice him into going to Mill Creek to do the deed. It was only fitting they made love for the first time there.

He'd never showed. The next morning she'd learned he left town, and her a short note. She'd cried for days, then lost her virginity to a classmate two months later. Not one of her finer moments, and she'd regretted nothing more than the rashness of her self-pity ever since.

But that was a lifetime ago. She was no longer that silly love-struck kid. She'd changed. He'd surely changed, too. Not that she thought he'd followed in his father's footsteps. She agreed with Mrs. Wilson. Matt was good to his core. He'd never be like his bitter despicable old man.

"Okay, this has crossed over to torture territory," Jamie whispered when Sally stepped away to grab a towel. "After our hair is done, you still want to get a manicure?"

"No."

Jamie grinned. "That was emphatic."

They'd already had to wait for the color to process then had their hair shampooed between numerous interruptions. A slew of customers stopped in to make appointments but mostly to find out if the news of Matt's return had hit The Cut and Curl yet.

With the water running close to her ear, Rachel hadn't heard much but then the disappointed faces told her enough. Twice she'd had to consciously stop clenching her teeth because, jeez, it was a shame to have suffered through two years of braces for nothing. "Our blow-outs shouldn't take long, but I swear, if Sally turns off that blow-dryer one more time so she can chitchat I'll scream."

"If anyone else walks in, that's exactly what she's going to do." Jamie turned to Roxy, who was trying to listen under the pretense of finding the right brush. "Let's keep this quick, huh? And we're skipping the manicures."

When Sally returned with the dry towel, after stopping to

yak with two more clients, Jamie passed on the same instructions to her. Rachel bit back a smile when the older woman gave Jamie a who-died-and-made-you-queen look that she completely ignored.

Jamie settled the tab while Rachel said her goodbyes. They stepped outside under the glaring afternoon sun, looked at each other and burst out laughing. The blue streak woven through Jamie's pretty tawny-colored hair was almost neon and wider than she'd had in mind.

"Purple suits you," Jamie said between snorts of laughter.

Rachel touched her hair. "I wanted out of there so badly I forgot to check it out."

"Don't you worry—it's very you." Jamie started giggling again.

"Gee, thanks for the endorsement. Do me a favor…make sure I'm there when Cole sees your hair."

She sniffed. "He'll love it."

"Yeah, right." Rachel glanced down Main Street. "Exactly what I was thinking."

"Would he still be in town?"

She swung her attention back to Jamie. "Cole?"

"No," Jamie said. "Uh-uh, don't you dare play dumb with me. Not after I had to sit there and keep my mouth shut for two hours." She checked for traffic, then tugged Rachel into the street. "Come on. You can tell me all about Matt at the Watering Hole."

"Keep your voice down." There wasn't a soul within earshot, but still… "I wish there was something to tell. But there isn't." On the next block she saw a silver truck she didn't recognize but then an older man opened the driver's door. "And please, your mouth was barely shut for ten minutes."

Jamie slid her a look of amusement. "I ought to get you drunk. Then let's see what comes through the floodgates."

"Nope. Won't happen." It suddenly occurred to her this

would be a crummy time to see him. Too many people around. Though surely he was gone by now.

A few barbs later they made it to the Watering Hole. Jamie muttered a mild curse when she couldn't open the door. "I can't believe it's closed."

"Try again. Sometimes it sticks." Rachel cast a final look down Main.

And held her breath when she saw him.

Matt was across the street at the other end of the block, coming out of the Food Mart. His hair looked darker and longer, still a light brown but without the sun streaks she'd always envied. He seemed taller, too, but that was probably her imagination.

"Is that him?" Jamie had won her battle with the door, and she stood there with it partially open, darting looks between Rachel and Matt.

"Yes." Rachel's voice came out a squeak and she cleared her throat as she watched him approach a black truck, a popular color around Blackfoot Falls. "It is."

"Wow. He looks yummy. Go say hi."

"No. I mean, I will." Dammit, her voice still sounded funny. "But not now."

Sadie, the owner, yelled from inside the bar for them to shut the door and quit letting out the heat. Jamie pulled it closed.

"We can't stay out here." Feeling jittery again, Rachel turned away from Matt and motioned for Jamie to get moving. "Go."

She wouldn't budge, only frowned in Matt's direction. "Who's that?"

Rachel couldn't resist, and saw a slender woman with long black hair come from behind Matt. He held the passenger door open for her, then helped her up into the cab.

"Do you know who she is?" Jamie murmured.

"No." Rachel swallowed. It was perfectly reasonable to assume Matt had taken the big step. He'd always struck her as the marrying kind. Except in her foolish young mind it had been her standing at the altar with him. "Okay, let's get me drunk."

MATT SLIPPED ON his sunglasses and drove down Main Street like a horse wearing blinders. He looked straight ahead, glad Nikki didn't feel the need to talk. Three years ago when he'd come to see his mother, he'd stayed away from town. He liked most of the people who lived in Blackfoot Falls just fine. But all the questions…Christ, they drove him nuts.

Mostly their interest was aimed at his rodeo career. He'd done well in the past six years, won titles and buckles, banked a small fortune in prize money, and the attention came with the territory. Early on he'd promised himself he'd never let his head get too big for his hat. A couple of veteran bronc riders on the circuit had been prime examples of how having a few extra bucks in your pocket could change a man. Turn him into someone he'd end up despising down the road.

Like Wallace. Except his father had always been miserable and cantankerous as far back as Matt could recall, and not just with him. Wallace's bad temper had extended to his wife, Matt's mother, and that he'd found intolerable. But she'd refused to leave the bastard, which Matt had never understood, and never would.

And now the miserable buzzard was sick, and Matt could honestly say he didn't give a damn. Any feelings he'd once had for the man had disappeared years ago. Matt had only come back for Nikki. She was confused and angry and needed closure before the old man kicked the bucket.

There was also the issue of the Lone Wolf. The ranch had been in the family for over a hundred and thirty years. According to the trust, the land had to be passed to another Gunderson. Whether the old man acknowledged her or not, Nikki had a right to half of everything. Gunderson blood flowed through her veins, and as far as Matt was concerned, she could have the whole operation—the land, the house, all of it. The place had been profitable, assuming Wallace hadn't run it into the ground, and Nikki needed the money. Needed to quit the dive bars she'd been working, maybe get herself an education.

The week before she died, his mother had told him about Nikki. He'd finally met her a year ago in Houston, and sometimes it was still hard to believe he had a sister. Officially she was his half sister, but so what? She was related to him by blood…. She was family. *His sister* without the technical bullshit attached. And he wanted the best for her.

Even if it meant facing the crazy old drunk a final time. Matt only hoped there was enough left of the Lone Wolf to give Nikki a fresh start. But then Wallace would've had to crawl pretty far into the bottle to let the place deteriorate. Besides drinking and being mean, the other thing he did consistently was try to one-up the McAllisters.

Matt sucked in some air. Man, he couldn't think about them without picturing Rachel. He didn't expect to see her, and he was sorry about that. But someone as bright and pretty and outgoing as her wouldn't stick around Blackfoot Falls. Rachel had far too much going for her. He'd reminded himself of that a hundred times the night he left ten years ago. Later, it had been no surprise to find out she'd gone to college. If she hadn't, now that would've shocked him.

"You're tense," Nikki said. "If you've changed your mind, we can turn around right now, be back in Houston by tomorrow night."

Matt glanced over at her. Her knees were drawn to her chest and she rocked gently against the seat belt. "It's gonna be okay," he said.

"I'm serious. We don't have to do this. The bastard will probably deny he's my father and we'll have come for nothing."

From the first day he met her, Nikki had always referred to Wallace as 'the bastard.' Then one night, after four shots of tequila with beer backs, Matt pointed out that technically *she* was the bastard. Silence had stretched long enough for him to regret teasing her. But then she'd smacked his arm and they'd laughed so loud the bartender told them to shut up or leave.

"What are you smiling about?" she asked, nerves making her mild Texas drawl more pronounced.

"Just wondering what you're gonna call him." Matt rested his wrist on the steering wheel, letting his hand dangle. "You've got choices…Wallace…you stupid bastard…Mr. Gunderson. You should be thinking about these things."

"You jerk." Laughing, Nikki shoved his shoulder. "I never should've let you talk me into this." She hugged her knees again. "I wish we'd stopped at that bar in town. I could've used something to calm my nerves."

"Yeah, that was the Watering Hole. Or some people call it Sadie's. She owns the place. Nice lady, though I've only been in there once. I left Blackfoot Falls before I was legal."

"So why did you go in there? To get the stupid bastard?" She exhaled sharply. "Yeah, I decided. Stupid bastard works for me."

Matt smiled. "Something like that." Hard to forget that day his mother had sent him to find Wallace.

He'd just turned sixteen, and the new heifer was about to drop her calf prematurely. His mother had worried Wallace would be furious if he wasn't told. She was right, though Matt had known either way he was screwed. The minute Wallace caught sight of him walking into the bar he'd flown into a rage.

He hadn't gotten physical, but he'd ranted and cussed at Matt the entire ride home. That day, for the first time in his life, Matt had been tempted to beat the crap out of him. For his mom's sake he'd held his temper. She was the reason he hadn't packed his bags the day he graduated from high school two years later. When he'd eventually ended up leaving, it was damn ironic his decision had also been because of her.

Nikki finally settled back in the leather seat and stared out her window. Except for the Rocky Mountains in the distance, there wasn't much to see on the road to the Lone Wolf. Especially in February with the ground patchy with snow. Once they turned north there'd be more trees and hills to liven the landscape.

"You disappointed there isn't more snow?" he asked after a while. She hadn't been this quiet since they stopped in Oklahoma.

"A little." She motioned with her chin. "Why is there so much more on the mountains?"

"Higher elevation." When he was a kid he never counted on seeing the dirt until late March. At times they'd be buried up to their knees with snow. But it was warmer this year than most.

Or so people had claimed in the Food Mart after their questions got too personal and he'd froze them out. They were all curious about Nikki, of course, but he'd refused to oblige them. He'd introduced her as a friend. No need for anyone to know who she was until they saw how the meeting with Wallace played out.

"Pretty country," she said. "Not flat like Houston."

"Yeah, I do miss the mountains. Hey, you know it could still snow later tonight or tomorrow." He knew she wanted to see it falling. "Don't let the blue skies fool you."

Her lips lifted in a faint smile. "You think we'll be here that long?"

"Yep," he said, but he'd hesitated a moment longer than he should've, and she sighed. The thing was, he truly didn't see them turning around too fast. If only because it might take a few rounds to knock some sense into Wallace's thick skull. "You want to play a word game?"

"No," she said, laughing and groaning at the same time. "You really have to learn to lose gracefully."

"Dammit, I didn't lose. We're tied." They'd played every car game he knew, mostly to distract her. Though he had to admit she'd surprised him. She was clever, street-smart if not book-smart, but she also understood people. Once she took a man's measure, she wasn't far off the mark. "We're about ten minutes out. Any more questions before we get there?"

She straightened her legs, putting her feet on the floor-board, then pulled her shoulders back as if ready to do battle. It wouldn't come to that. Matt wouldn't let it. "You still don't think we should call first?"

"Nope." He wasn't as confident on taking that stand. Some-where between the Food Mart and his truck, it struck him that he could've called Lucy to give her a heads-up and get one him-self. The woman wasn't just a housekeeper, she was a saint.

He knew she was still tending to Wallace three days a week, even though she was getting on in years. She'd been hired a month before Matt was born, had witnessed more than a few of Wallace's tirades and had been a champ through his moth-er's illness.

Yep, he probably should've called Lucy. Hell.

Too late now.

They were officially on Gunderson land, the place he'd sworn he'd never come back to.

3

WALLACE WAS DRUNK. Passed out on the old rawhide couch in his office, his jaw slack, his graying hair poking out every which way. Half a bottle of Jim Beam sat on the wood floor an inch from where his arm dangled off to the side.

Staring at him in disgust, Matt was glad he'd left Nikki in the truck. She didn't need to see this; no one did. Matt breathed in deep, wondering how many times his mother had to walk in to find her worthless husband sprawled out, spittle dried at the corners of his mouth. Wallace hadn't been this bad the first time Matt had put Blackfoot Falls in his rearview mirror.

Even so, a couple times he'd walked in when his mother had just shaken out a blanket over the old man. She'd tucked it around him and kissed his forehead, then went to bed by herself. It killed Matt that she was so patient and tolerant. He hadn't understood then, and never would get why she'd stayed in the marriage. He'd begged her to leave Wallace. But she'd always just smiled, said she loved him and maybe someday he'd change.

Then Matt found out about Wallace's affair with Rosa Flores. From his own mother. She'd known for over fifteen years, even that a child was involved. And still she'd stayed. Now she was gone, and Matt missed her, missed their secret phone calls. He missed the garbled texts she'd sent him from the smartphone he'd bought her so they could communicate without Wallace knowing.

He smiled, thinking about how she'd never gotten the hang of texting or sending emails. She'd sure liked getting his, though, and quickly figured out how to read them.

There were still days when Matt struggled against his anger. At her. Sometimes at himself. Always at Wallace. No one could convince Matt the stress of living with the bastard hadn't shortened her life.

She'd claimed she loved Wallace. Love. What the hell did that word mean? It was supposed to be something good. Something that made you happy, stronger, passionate…even country songs touted its virtue. But obviously love could also make you stupid.

Matt ran his gaze over his father's frail form. He seemed shorter, narrower, definitely not the same big man who'd doggedly bullied Matt over schoolwork, how he rode a horse or mucked the stables. Sometimes Wallace had scared the crap out of him.

Funny, he thought, watching the drool slip from a corner of Wallace's open mouth, he'd been worried his hatred of the man would seep out like venom in front of Nikki. But Matt actually felt pity seeing him lie there, his life nothing but a wasteland. The letter Matt had received from his mother's friend about Wallace being sick hadn't mentioned the diagnosis. Matt assumed it was either cancer or cirrhosis, but he didn't know.

Hell, maybe the booze helped dull the pain.

Cursing at himself, Matt scooped the fallen magazines off the floor and tossed them onto the oak coffee table. What the hell was he doing making excuses for the old drunk? That logic didn't wash anyway. He'd been a drinker since Matt was a small kid.

He glanced around at the used glasses and opened mail that

littered the desk and table. Obviously it was Lucy's day off or the place would've been tidier. He was kind of glad since he would've hurt her feelings by not calling ahead. No sense in him cleaning up. He wouldn't bring Nikki in here, not with Wallace passed out like this. Matt wanted the man sober, clear-headed enough that he might use the chance to do right by Nikki and give her some answers.

After closing the office door, Matt surveyed the family room, then stuck his head in the kitchen. The rest of the house seemed okay. He doubted anyone had recently used the guest room where he planned on putting Nikki. Knowing Lucy, she kept it dusted, and if not, the room would still be better than the dingy one-bedroom apartment Nikki called home.

He walked outside to where his truck waited in front of the house. The sky was getting dark and he couldn't see Nikki through the tinted windows, but he knew she was there. She wouldn't have gotten out of the cab.

To the left of the barn the long rectangular bunkhouse was lit up. It was suppertime for the men, which had been part of Matt's arrival plan. Several hired hands had been with the Lone Wolf for over twenty years. They knew their jobs, and Wallace left them alone. Matt liked one of the old-timers in particular, but he hadn't wanted to run into anyone before he'd seen Wallace.

Nikki cracked the door open when he got close. "What's going on?" she asked, her voice nervous. "You were gone a long time."

"Sorry," he said glancing at his watch.

"So? Are we staying or leaving?"

"Staying." He opened the back door of the extended cab to get their bags.

He noticed her gaze stray toward the house, but she didn't make a move to get out. He'd turned on a foyer lamp but he should've flipped on a couple more. The place was big, two and a half stories, with lots of natural stone and wood, and looking eerie in the dusky twilight. It was a well-built home constructed in the 1920s after the original log cabin burned to the ground.

"What did he say about you being here?" she asked, pushing the door open all the way.

"He's asleep." He paused. "Maybe drunk." Matt yanked out the small duffel he'd brought, annoyed at himself for pussy-footing around the truth. But unlike his mother, he wasn't trying to protect Wallace. Matt sighed. It wasn't like she wouldn't know…. "He is drunk. Doubt he'll be waking up anytime soon."

She stared at the house, still gripping the door handle. "We can't just go in there."

"Yeah, we can. It's my house, too." He almost added it was equally hers, but she didn't like hearing anything to do with the Trust or her being a Gunderson. "We'll get you settled in the guest room, then put something together for dinner. We'll have the kitchen to ourselves." He saw how thrilled she was with that idea. "Or go eat at the diner in town. Up to you."

She quietly closed her door and reached around him for the bag of bread, cold cuts and cheese they'd bought at the Food Mart. "I'm not hungry, but I vote we go out."

"Okay." He grabbed her bag with his other hand and used his elbow to close the truck door. "After we eat I have to make a stop. Another ranch not too far from here called the Sundance."

"Tonight?"

They walked side by side toward the porch. "Yeah, I probably should." No need to point out they could be headed back to Texas come morning. He didn't think so, though the possibility existed. But he couldn't leave without seeing Barbara McAllister. He owed her a debt, and he aimed to pay it.

"I SHOULD WAIT IN THE TRUCK," Nikki murmured as they walked toward the McAllister house, all lit up as if there might be a party inside.

"You'll like them. You won't meet nicer people." He bumped her shoulder. "Three brothers, all good-looking guys."

"Bet they're flattered you noticed."

Matt shook his head, sliding her an irritated look. Truthfully he was glad she'd relaxed enough to joke around. Meeting genuine folks like the McAllisters would help make her more comfortable and give her a better feeling for Blackfoot Falls. He'd mentioned that it would be safe to tell them she was his sister, but she wasn't ready and insisted that she be introduced as a friend.

They got to the porch and he looked over at her. "How you doing, sis? You okay?"

She wasn't shy or timid, but she always blushed a little when he called her *sis*. Tossing her hair back, she eyed the big glass window. "You country people have some weird customs. Someone shows up at my door without calling, I don't answer."

"Uh, yeah, I know."

"And yet you've learned nothing."

Ignoring her sigh, he got a good look inside as they mounted the steps. Not that he'd admit it, but he suddenly had second thoughts about the surprise visit. There were a lot of people moving around the living room, mostly young women. Just his luck Mrs. McAllister was having a Tupperware party or some damn thing like that.

"We can still turn around," Nikki whispered.

"Nah." He knocked on the door, waited, heard the music and laughter inside, and tried again, only louder.

"Still think this is a good time?"

He stepped back. "Maybe not."

The door opened. A blonde he didn't know smiled at them.

She had a drink in one hand, and waved them inside with the other. "Come in."

He looked past her, hoping to see Cole or Trace, anyone he recognized. At least half a dozen women were sitting in the living room sipping drinks near the fireplace, and several more stood toward the back. They were all dressed up, some of them wearing fancy sweaters, high-heeled city boots and skintight pants. Like they were vacationing at one of those pricey ski lodges. Nobody looked familiar.

His gaze caught on a nice ass in a pair of worn jeans, small waist…

He blinked hard at the loose auburn curls that skimmed her shoulders. Only one woman he knew had hair that deep sexy reddish-brown shade.

She turned around. Her gaze connected with his and her green eyes widened. The smile slipped from her pink lips. She looked exactly how he felt. Stunned. "Matt?"

"Rachel?" he said at the same time. "What are you doing here?"

"Me?" She handed her drink to the blonde still standing at the door. "I live here," Rachel said with a strained laugh as she wiped her palms down her jeans. "Come on in."

Man, he hadn't expected this. But he really had no choice but to stay. Best he could do was keep it short. Turning around now would make him look like a damn fool.

His feet couldn't seem to move. "Hey, I can come back tomorrow. Obviously you're having a party. I should've called."

Behind him Nikki snorted.

Rachel smiled at her. "Get in here, Matthew Gunderson, so I can close the door, and you can make an introduction."

Sighing, he stomped his boots on the mat, shaking off loose gravel and dried mud, then tried to let Nikki go first but she gave her head a small shake.

"It's so nice to see you, Matt," Rachel said as soon as he

and Nikki stepped inside. After hesitating a moment, Rachel gave him a hug.

His arms automatically came up around her, and he prayed she couldn't feel his heart pounding against his chest. The embrace was brief, somewhat awkward, as if it was fulfilling an obligation and not something she wanted to do.

Maybe it was his fault. He might've held her a little too tight. Exhaling slowly, he moved farther back, hoping to erase any wrong signal on his part.

"I'm Rachel," she said to Nikki, who then introduced herself, since Matt's dry mouth couldn't seem to work. "And don't worry, it's not a party, not really," Rachel said, talking fast, her pitch higher than he remembered. "Let's go find my brothers. Would you like a drink?"

Nikki looked to him for an answer, the question in her eyes plain. Staying or leaving? Finally she said, "I'll take a beer if you have one."

"We do, in addition to wine, margaritas and a weird punch my brother concocted—" Rachel caught him staring at her. She blinked, glanced away, then returned her gaze to him, a stubborn glint in her eyes he knew well. "What?"

"Your hair." He chuckled. "It's purple—"

"Oh." Her hand shot up to touch her head, and she blushed.

"God, Matt." Nikki glared at him. "It's the style."

"I know. But Rachel's not the type to…" Hell, what did he know? Apparently nothing, judging by the way both women stared at him. Nikki's brown eyes told him he was a jerk for having laughed. Rachel didn't seem embarrassed anymore, but somewhat amused.

"Let's go get your drinks," Rachel said, giving her hair a toss as if to say, "yeah, it's purple, so what?" and then leading them in the direction of the dining room.

That was something else he remembered about her. Whenever she got embarrassed or tongue-tied she recovered quickly.

He'd envied her that neat trick. Not him. Once he got bucked outta the saddle, he had a heck of a time thinking on his feet. After winning a bunch of titles and having so many microphones shoved in his face, he would've thought he'd be better at a comeback.

"It really is a party," someone whispered from behind.

He turned his head. It was the blonde from the door. She was following them.

With a flirty smile, she leaned closer. "It's Rachel's birthday."

Matt shot a look back at Rachel. He'd known the date, but he'd totally forgotten. Probably blocked it out. He'd never regretted leaving Blackfoot Falls, but he had regretted leaving Rachel…the day before her sixteenth birthday.

If Rachel had to smile for a minute longer, her face was going to split in half. Or crack. Or do something equally unattractive. The second she'd heard Matt was in town she knew she'd see him at some point, but she hadn't expected him to knock on her door.

Wow, she wished she hadn't let Trace talk her into a glass of the lethal punch he'd cooked up. Especially not after the tequila shots earlier with Jamie. Her head was spinning, she was jabbering like a hormonal parrot, and good God, if her voice squeaked any higher she'd have to pass out earplugs.

Her best defense was to find her brothers. They'd keep Matt busy talking. Of course the subject of Matt had come up at dinner and she'd learned that Trace and Cole had been following his rodeo career. According to them, he'd made quite a name for himself…. He was like a rock star in the sport of bull riding.

She vaguely recalled her mother mentioning he'd started rodeoing seven years ago. Apparently Rachel hadn't been in the mood to hear about him. It wasn't until she moved away that she could think of him with any objectivity. And then it hadn't mattered because after the homesickness passed, she'd adapted quickly to college life. Yes, she'd enjoyed coming home for the holidays, but she was always ready to return to her independence and the lights of Dallas.

Still, she wondered if he'd ever understood how badly he'd crushed her tender heart. Probably not. At the time he thought she was too young for him. It was more likely that he'd passed her affection off as a phase that had faded within a week.

She stopped at the dining room table, covered with filled ice buckets, glasses, chilling wine and a big bowl of Trace's pinkish-orange punch sitting next to the leftover birthday cake. The lettering was mostly gone and you couldn't tell the cake was for her. She was glad about that. Though not so happy to see that the beer hadn't been replenished in the silver cooler.

"Okay," she said, picking up glasses and holding them up to the light just to be sure they were clean. "We have more beer in the family room wet bar, also a blender of margarita mix in the kitchen. And this? My brother's 100 proof…frankly, I'm not sure what to call it. He says punch."

"Let me guess…." Matt smiled. "Trace?"

Rachel nodded. "He was only seventeen when you left, and still you know."

Matt's smile faded. The cautious way he met her eyes removed any doubt he was thinking about that night—him leaving, not saying a word, the inadequate note he'd left for her….

If they were alone she'd tell him it was okay. He didn't have to worry. It wouldn't be a lie, but seeing each other again after all those years was stirring up crazy and unexpected feelings. At least for her.

Oh, God…an annoying thought struck her. She'd done the math. She could've made any sort of joke about Trace not changing. Most people wouldn't remember it had been exactly ten years since Matt left. But she did. Ten years and one day.

Jeez, what was wrong with her? Until she'd seen him earlier, she really hadn't been thinking about him. Even if she had, too bad. He had Nikki. And she was gorgeous with her long dark hair, olive skin and light brown eyes.

"So…" Rachel pretended to study the table and cleared her throat. "What will it be?"

"I've changed my mind about the beer," Nikki said. "I might need the punch." She glanced at Matt, who eyed her with a touch of amusement and an almost imperceptible shake of his head.

Their private look depressed Rachel. It shouldn't have— she had no business having any reaction. Carefully keeping her gaze lowered, she grabbed the tongs to put ice in the glass.

"I can do that myself," Nikki said. "Matt, I know you want a beer, so why don't you two go get it. I'll find you."

Rachel looked up. He was watching her with blue eyes she remembered differently. Had she been too young to notice the smoldering intensity? "Beer?"

"Unless your brothers wiped them out."

"They better not have." She moved around the table, smiling at Nikki. "Help yourself to the cake. Or anything in the kitchen," she added, feeling a bit guilty.

It would make sense to wait for her since it took seconds to ladle punch into a glass. But Rachel wanted Matt to herself, even if only for two minutes.

"Thanks," Nikki said. "The cake does look good. I just might have a piece."

Matt's brows drew together in a puzzled frown directed at Nikki, who ignored him and switched places with Rachel so she could get to the punch bowl.

"You want to wait for her?" Rachel asked, unnerved to be near enough to see a small scar on his beard-roughened chin.

"Nah, she's okay. I never have to worry about that one."

Except he did, Rachel could see it in his lingering gaze, and she felt horrible for being disappointed. But when he touched the small of her back as she slipped past him, she felt something else altogether.

It was crazy, inappropriate, unacceptable, yet she couldn't make herself unfeel the sizzling electric shock that had flowed from his palm up her spine. She sincerely hoped it was the cumulative effect of the day's booze causing her to act like a dope. She wasn't the type of woman to covet a man who was taken. He was with Nikki, though Rachel didn't believe they were married, and not just because of the lack of rings. It was simply a gut feeling. Had she kept her mouth shut instead of babbling when she first saw them, he would've introduced Nikki himself.

"I don't know any of these people, do I?"

Rachel started. It wasn't his question that made her jump, but the proximity of his mouth to her ear…his warm breath gliding over her skin. She'd already led him through the living room without realizing it. The guests were all staring at him—of course they were, they were women.

Her birthday celebration had included them, and they'd heard the dinner talk. Now they were putting two and two together, and they were checking out the hot, sexy rodeo star.

"You don't," she said, pausing to clear her head enough to ensure her voice and brain were in sync. Obviously he didn't know about the dude ranch part of the Sundance. "So much has happened just in the past year…."

They had to sidestep Carla, a guest from Indianapolis, who blocked their path to the family room. She got in a breathy, "Hi," aimed at Matt before they could pass her.

"Evenin'," he said, giving her a polite smile.

"Have some cake, Carla," Rachel said pleasantly, but stayed on course. She tilted her head closer to Matt. "We're going to keep walking or else you can forget about your beer."

"Yeah, I know," he said, which probably shouldn't have

made Rachel smile because his grim tone indicated he might be sick of too much female attention at this point in his career.

She wondered how he'd handled the buckle-bunny phenomena. Although the rodeo scene had never interested her, she knew about the groupies who followed the circuit. It didn't matter if the guy was attractive. If he was at the top of his game, he was getting a whole lot of hotel room keys stuffed in his pockets.

For Matt, it had to be a double whammy. He'd always been good-looking with his sun-lightened hair and beautiful blue eyes. It wasn't just her opinion. Half the girls in high school, all four grades, had secretly crushed on him. Yet he'd only had one girlfriend. They'd both been sophomores, as serious as two fifteen-year-olds can be…until his father had humiliated him in front of Emily and then ran her off the Lone Wolf.

Now, almost thirty, Matt was even better-looking than he'd been at nineteen. The years had given his face more character, with fine lines at the outside corners of his eyes, grooves along his sexy mouth that apparently she'd been unable to suitably appreciate in her youth. His nose seemed different, though, a bit crooked.

"Rachel, wait." He caught her arm just outside the family room.

Her heart nearly stopped. Had he noticed her staring? If he felt compelled to point out he was with Nikki and not interested in straying, Rachel would just die. Right here. Right now, on her twenty-sixth birthday. So sad.

She did as he asked, but he didn't let go. Staring into each other's eyes, they stood in a small semi-private foyer that was the result of an addition to the original house.

Matt smiled. "It's good to see you." He stroked his palm down her arm to her hand, and lightly squeezed.

"Yeah, you, too."

"I'm sorry I didn't remember."

"What?"

He lowered his head, slowly closing the distance between their mouths.

Rachel sucked in a breath so hard she thought she'd pass out. Holy crap, he was going to kiss her....

He moved his head, just a tad, and pressed a kiss to her cheek. "Happy birthday, kiddo."

4

RACHEL DIDN'T CARE THAT he was so handsome he made her thighs clench. Or that there were far too many witnesses in the next room. She was going to strangle him.

Kiddo.

A barely contained growl chafed her throat. This was like adding the proverbial salt to the wound.

He had to know…the way he'd leaned into her…the dark intensity of his eyes…well, naturally she'd expected an entirely different kind of kiss.

Dammit, she didn't understand this grown-up version of Matt at all. Her teasing and flirting used to earn her slow bashful smiles. She'd enjoyed having the upper hand.

Or had she? As a kid had she gotten his reaction to her mixed up? Maybe those smiles had been patronizing. Her breath caught painfully somewhere between her lungs and her throat.

"Thanks," she said, smiled brightly and led him into the family room, announcing, "Look who's here."

Cole and Trace both glanced up from their game of pool. Jamie was there, too. Just in case Jamie was making faces at her, Rachel kept her eyes averted.

"Hey, Matt." Cole leaned his stick against the wall, and

stuck out his hand as he came around the table. "Good to see you, buddy."

Trace passed his cue to Sandy, a pretty blonde who'd checked in yesterday. Her quieter friend, Krista, was already holding Trace's beer.

"I should've known you hustlers were back here." Matt shook each of their hands, and acknowledged the women with a polite nod.

"Hustlers, huh?" Sandy baited Trace, while she discreetly sized up Matt.

"Now that's what you call sour grapes. Matt can't play worth spit. We used to humiliate him."

"Yep." Matt laughed. "I still suck at it." He stuffed his hands in his jeans' pockets and leaned a shoulder against the wall. "You guys still keep a running score?"

Cole snorted, and eyed Trace. "No. Some of us are busy and don't have enough time to play these days."

"Translation…" Trace said with a cocky smile, "I'm still whipping him."

Leaping to Cole's defense, Jamie let out a haughty "You do not."

"That's my girl." Chuckling, Cole caught her hand. "Matt, this is Jamie."

"I see things have changed around here." Matt briefly raised his brows at Cole. "Nice meeting you, Jamie."

"Yes, likewise."

"Now you know why my brother has no time for pool." Trace reclaimed the cue from Sandy. She gave him a stiff smile and a pointed look. "Oh, yeah, Matt, this—" Trace paused, a fleeting expression of panic on his face. "You want a beer?" Trace didn't wait for the answer. He flashed a winning smile at the tall blonde. "Darlin', you mind getting Matt a cold one?"

"Sure."

Rachel and Jamie exchanged glances. They knew Trace had

already forgotten the woman's name. Rachel pressed her lips together and lowered her gaze to the eight ball in the corner, trying not to laugh. She should bail him out. Not to be nice, he deserved to squirm, but it wasn't fair to let their guests feel uncomfortable.

She moved around the pool table and picked up two empty glasses sitting on the window ledge. "Sandy, Krista, would you like another drink?"

"Not me, thanks." Krista exhaled loudly. "Trace's punch nearly did me in."

"Amen," Sandy added, pulling a bottle out of the small fridge.

"Yeah," Rachel said. "I don't think we'll let him play bartender again." Okay, she'd done her part. Let Trace figure out who was who.

Matt pushed off the wall to take the beer Sandy passed him. "Thanks." He gave her a smile that could melt a brick. "I don't recall so many pretty women in Blackfoot Falls before I left."

"Handsome and charming." Sandy's smile dazzled. "Why did I not know this about Montana men?"

Rachel tried really hard not to roll her eyes. Good thing.

Sandy glanced at her. "There's only one beer left. I'll restock if you tell me where to get more."

"You're a guest. I'll get it."

"No, it's your birthday," Jamie cut in. "They're in the kitchen. Sandy and Krista, come help me."

With the other two trailing behind her, Jamie walked past Rachel and gave her an OMG look no one else could see.

"Well, shit," Trace said as soon as the women were out of earshot. "Look at you, Gunderson, making the ladies hot and bothered. You don't get enough action on the road?"

"You seem to be doing okay," Matt said, laughing. "And you don't have to get thrown from a bull."

"But he's sure been flinging a lot of it around," Cole said, and took his next shot.

Trace glanced toward the door. "Hell, those women are wearing me out. No joke."

Rachel grunted. "They just arrived yesterday."

"You know what I mean." Trace took a swig of beer. "Good time for you to show up, Matt. You'll take the heat off."

"Oh, please, you're not fooling anyone." Rachel knew it was true. Trace had gotten sick of the attention. But she wanted to steer the conversation away from Matt and his sex life. Just the hint of it grated on her nerves. "You've been the main attraction. I really should pay you a bonus."

"No, thanks. What I need is time off for damn good behavior."

Cole laughed at that. "I don't think you want to go down that road." He eyed Trace as if he knew something Rachel didn't. Did Cole honestly believe she didn't know Trace had played loose with the rules? She suspected he'd slept with a guest or three in the past few months, but he'd been discreet. "Your shot." Cole stood back to give Trace room and looked at Matt. "I reckon you came to see your father."

He hesitated, then took a long pull of beer. "Yeah, I'm here because of Wallace. Where's Jesse?"

Clearly Matt wanted the subject of his father dropped. "He's away overnight," Rachel said. "In Wyoming, I think. He's an animal-rescue volunteer."

"Good for him."

No one said anything while Trace crouched, squinting at the eight ball, trying to line up his next shot. A giddy laugh from the living room distracted him. He missed and cursed under his breath.

"What's going on around here?" Matt asked. "Who are these women?"

"Wow, that's right, you don't know about our new venture."

Rachel sighed. "I started to tell you earlier. We're trying our hand at the dude ranch business."

"Not we," Trace said.

Rachel gave him the evil eye.

Matt frowned, processing the information, then turned and swung a look toward the living room. "Why?"

"Money," Rachel said quietly. "This economy has been tough on ranchers." She shrugged, and glanced over her shoulder to make sure no guests were within earshot. "This won't be forever."

Cole and Trace had already returned to their game, but Matt looked troubled. Thoughtfully sipping his beer, he kept his gaze on the pool table, but his mind was obviously working overtime. This wasn't the time or place to get into this particular topic. Not that she ever wanted to discuss the family's financial woes with Matt or anyone.

While he was distracted by her brothers, it was nice to have a few minutes to check him out. His chest was broader now, so were his shoulders. He'd always been lean with just enough muscle to make her want to skim her palms over his chest and back. But he was a bull rider now. And staying on such a powerful animal required strength and balance. It meant being in top physical condition. Matt looked the part.

She drew in a long slow breath, her gaze falling to his exposed forearms. He'd turned back the sleeves of his navy blue shirt since he'd come inside or else she would've noticed all that sleek corded muscle before now. Even the denim couldn't hide his strong thighs, and God, she really had to stop looking.

"I was hoping I'd find y'all back here."

Nikki's voice startled her. Rachel abruptly turned to the door, guilt warming her cheeks because she'd completely forgotten about the woman. "Oh, good, you found us," Rachel said lamely.

"This is a cool house." Nikki smiled, not looking as though

she felt neglected or annoyed. She had a beer in her hand, not in a glass but the bottle, half of it already gone.

"Hey, Nik." Matt held a hand out to her, and she slipped past Rachel to go to his side.

"Hi," she said to Cole and Trace before Matt could introduce them—probably because they'd both stopped playing to look at her. Trace automatically set down his cue.

"This is my friend, Nikki," Matt said, then pointed his bottle. "That's Cole. And Trace."

Okay, he'd said friend, not wife, though Rachel had already decided they weren't married. But did friend mean girlfriend? Friend with benefits? What?

"Y'all are Rachel's brothers." Nikki shook back her shiny sable hair, a practical gesture and not the least flirty. But then she was one of those women who would look sexy flossing her teeth. "I've heard a lot about you."

"Hello, Nikki." Cole set aside his beer just as Jamie appeared holding a six-pack in each hand and cradling one to her side. "And that's Jamie, my better half."

"We've already met," Nikki said, passing her bottle to Matt and then taking the extra six-pack from Jamie. "You should've told me…I would've helped."

Rachel started to jump in but realized they didn't need her. That didn't stop Trace from rushing to the fridge ahead of them and opening the door. He crouched in front of the two empty bottom shelves letting Jamie pass him the bottles, which he laid on their sides to maximize space.

"You putting anything else in here?" he asked before getting up. The question was meant for Jamie and Rachel, but his gaze lingered on Nikki.

He was cool about it, not making an ass out of himself, or being obvious, but Rachel knew him too well. For one thing, as willing as he was to help when she asked for it, he wasn't one to volunteer.

"Sandy and Krista are bringing two more," Jamie said. "But I think they took a detour first."

Trace nodded and straightened. Rachel saw the set of his jaw and knew he'd forgotten about the other two and probably hoped they stayed detoured.

The room was spacious even with the massive stone fireplace, pool table, overstuffed leather couch and club chairs. But the way the furniture was set up, if you weren't playing pool, you either stood and watched or sat by the fire. It had never been a problem when it was just the family, but since taking in guests who often converged here after dinner, Rachel had to rethink the arrangement.

After their game was finished, Cole and Trace quit playing in favor of talking to Matt and Nikki. They moved to the couch and chairs along with Jamie, and the table was quickly claimed by a pair of wranglers who'd come in after dinner and were keeping the guests entertained.

Sandy and Krista seemed determined to stick close to Trace, and though Rachel could tell he was unhappy with the situation, there was really nothing she could do about it.

Three women had accompanied the wranglers, and a few minutes later, two more had wandered in to cheer the men on. With so many people squeezed in, the room was noisy and too warm, and making Rachel itchy for some fresh air and solitude. As soon as she could slip away, she picked up empty glasses and carried them to the kitchen.

Relieved to be alone, she opened the dishwasher. The sink had been clear an hour ago when her mom had gone to lie down because of a headache. But dishes and glasses had accumulated and Rachel started loading them, glad to be able to hear herself think. It had been one hell of a day…a birthday she wasn't likely to forget.

Matt Gunderson, here in the flesh. It still didn't seem real. Every time her gaze had touched on him she'd received a small jolt of awareness. One minute he'd laugh or turn his head a certain way, looking like the old Matt, and the next, he was a handsome stranger who made her pulse race.

She would have to look him up on Google later. Just out of curiosity. Whether the thing he had with Nikki was serious or not, Rachel was quite clear where she stood in his eyes. Damn, but she really wished he hadn't given her that peck on the cheek. If he hadn't, at least she could've fantasized about him a while longer.

"Need help?"

Matt.

Aware her butt was sticking up in the air as she tried to reach the back row of the dishwasher, she calmly deposited the plate in a suitable slot, then straightened.

When she turned around he didn't try to pretend he hadn't been checking out her ass. Which just confused her. "Good timing on your part. I'm almost done."

"You're the birthday girl. You shouldn't have kitchen duty."

She shrugged. "Just another day."

He set his empty bottle on the counter. "So you've stopped counting down right after Christmas?"

She smiled, surprised he remembered. "Every kid loves their birthday. I'm not a kid anymore."

"No," he said, his voice lowered, his gaze sweeping her lips. "You're not."

Rachel grabbed the dish towel off the counter, needing something to do. "You want another beer?"

"I've had two already. That's enough."

"I guess you have to keep yourself in good physical condition." It was a perfectly innocent and natural observation. Except she panned the breadth of his shoulders, and her lips parted without permission. "Where's Nikki?"

He motioned with his head. "She's still talking to your brothers and Jamie. Cole has himself a real sweetheart. I can tell she's good for him. He's lightened up."

"True. Jamie's terrific. I'm glad she's here. Wait a minute— You left Nikki with Trace?" She laughed. "Are you crazy?"

Matt grinned. "She can take care of herself."

"Yeah, but—" Rachel turned away.

He caught her chin and drew her eyes back to his. "There's nothing going on with Nikki and me. Okay?"

"None of my business." Oh, hell. She had to ask.... "Then why would you bring her home?"

He let his hand fall away, but continued to study her face. After a drawn-out silence, he said, "It's complicated."

"Fair enough." They were still standing close, and maybe she should've stepped back, but her brain was too busy processing this new information. He'd made a point of clarifying his relationship with Nikki.... "You sure don't owe me an explanation."

"There's a good one." He huffed out a short laugh. "But it's not up to me right now. What about you? Anyone special?"

"Here? In Blackfoot Falls? Uh...no." The condescension in her tone shamed her. Her brothers and Matt and lots of other men born and bred around the county were terrific guys and didn't deserve the thoughtless remark.

Matt's mouth quirked up on one side but he didn't appear to take offense. "Anywhere?"

"No." She bit her lip and fisted the dish towel. "That was a horrible thing for me to say. I didn't mean it."

He shrugged. "Frankly, I didn't expect you to be here."

"That, too, is complicated." She saw amusement enter his eyes. "That's not payback. I'm being serious."

"It seems we have some catching up to do." He lifted a lock of her hair, and she automatically moved closer. "Purple, huh?"

Oh, God, she'd forgotten. "Last year it was pink."

His brows rose slightly. "So how long does it last?"

"Depends on how much I want to annoy Cole and Jesse, or put up with Trace's crap."

"Ah." He smiled at her, really smiled, as if he was recalling fond memories of them sneaking off to Mill Creek.

They'd kissed there for the first time, and she wondered if he remembered. Not necessarily a good thing. She'd been horrifically inexperienced and it had taken a while for him to get her to relax. Turned out kissing a pair of warm lips was very different than practicing on the back of her hand.

With her luck, it was probably why he'd pecked her on the cheek earlier. That thought broke the warm fuzzy spell she'd been slipping under. She cleared her throat, moved back. "You're taller."

Matt blinked, the brief charged moment between them gone. "I think Trace and I were neck and neck when I left. He's passed me by."

"My brothers are giants. It's that McAllister gene." She stepped around him and closed the dishwasher door. "According to the family Bible, for five generations every McAllister male has topped out over six-two."

"Trace has gotta be about that. I'm six feet and he's not *that* much taller than me."

For a second, Rachel feared she'd misjudged what could've led to a nice sexy kiss. Why else were they having this pointless conversation? She doubted Matt's ego over being shorter than her brothers had anything to do with it. But then she barely knew Matt anymore. Knowing the boy didn't mean she knew the man. It kind of depressed her because the odds weren't in her favor. Who could say what success had done to him. In the rodeo world, a champion bull rider had status, money, more women than he knew what to do with. Matt was that guy now.

She rinsed out the sink, fine with letting the conversation lapse, but eventually she looked over at him.

He was leaning against the counter, watching her. "You take after your mom," he said quietly. "Petite and—"

"I'm not petite. I'm five-five."

"Whoa." He chuckled. "I didn't mean it as an insult."

She bit off a response. Nikki and Jamie entered the kitchen, carrying more empty glasses and bottles. Rachel smiled, trying not to be grumpy because she no longer had Matt to herself. It was a small miracle that they'd managed to be alone for the fifteen minutes.

As soon as Matt heard Nikki's voice, he straightened and picked up the bottle he'd left on the counter. "You recycle?"

Puzzled, Rachel nodded and pointed to the blue bin near the mudroom door. The question wasn't necessarily odd, but his tone was more impersonal. He wouldn't have lied about Nikki....

"Have you been cleaning up?" Jamie asked, depositing glasses in the sink. "Stop it. Today is supposed to be your day off."

"Right." Rachel sighed. "My mom has a headache so I'm pitching in."

"Put me to work," Nikki offered.

"No, but thanks." Rachel hung the towel. "The dishwasher is full. We can let it run while we rejoin the party."

Matt separated the new crop of bottles and carried them to the bin. "We need to shove off," he said, and Nikki nodded solemnly. "I wanted to see your mom," he said to Rachel. "Tell her I'll come by again, would you?"

"Sure." She tried not to look surprised, but she wasn't aware Matt and her mother knew each other well enough that he'd pay her a special visit. "I could get her now."

"No, don't. I'll be around for a while."

Nikki swung a startled look at him. Clearly, she had other ideas.

5

"SHE HASN'T GOTTEN over you," Nikki said, the moment they were bumping over the Sundance's gravel driveway, headed for the highway.

"Who?"

"Oh, come on. You know I mean Rachel. Who I like very much, by the way, so you have my blessing."

"Gee, thanks. I'm relieved." Matt shook his head. The beer hadn't mellowed him. He was irritable but couldn't figure out why, and Nikki wasn't helping. "To illustrate how little you know, she was sixteen when I left."

Nikki laughed. "So you never…got down and dirty with her?"

"Were you not listening? Rachel was sixteen, Nik. Jesus."

She sighed and let her head fall back against the headrest. "My brother, so honorable. Why can't I find someone like you?"

It was his turn to laugh. "Careful what you wish for. I thought I'd have to plug Trace's eyes back in his head when he saw you."

She let out an unladylike snort. "Guys like him? Uh-uh. Hot? Yes. But he knows it. Uses it. No, thank you. I've had my share of those dogs. No more. I'm done."

"You're sure about that?" Remarkably cheered, Matt glanced over at her. "Because I don't think you made yourself clear."

She brought her head up. "You're an ass."

Matt just smiled. She'd called him worse. "I think you're wrong about Trace."

"Are you kidding me? Didn't you see the way he was flirting with those two women?"

"I saw him being polite. The blonde was doing the flirting. But I reckon it doesn't matter."

"No, it doesn't," she murmured and stared off mutely into the darkness beyond her window. A few seconds later she asked, "How far away are we?"

"Fifteen minutes."

"Want to go to the Watering Hole?"

"You're gonna turn into a drunk trying to put off meeting Wallace."

"So?" She paused. "What do you think? Watering Hole?"

"I'm not dying to see him either, you know."

"Yeah, I do." She fidgeted a minute, and then turned on the radio. Only garbled voices blasted from the speakers, so she obsessively pressed buttons.

The connection was poor this far east of Kalispell. He'd already told her earlier. "You won't find anything." He tugged at his collar, trying to loosen it. She was making him edgy. Coming out of nowhere, it struck him. "The chocolate cake— I finally got it."

She turned off the annoying static. "What are you talking about?"

"You hate chocolate cake. I'd wondered what you were up to.... You were giving Rachel and me time alone."

"So? I'm a thoughtful sister." She reached for the knob again.

"Then you won't mind leaving the damn radio off."

Sighing, she slumped back. "You're the only person I know who doesn't keep CDs in their car."

He ignored her and flicked on the brights. The moon hid behind an overcast sky and it was pitch-black all around them. "Rachel and I were friends. We used to go swimming at a creek up the hill behind the Lone Wolf."

"Doesn't mean she didn't have the hots for you."

Matt smiled. "Yeah, we had a mutual appreciation for each other. But mostly, we were friends."

Nikki groaned. "Did you ever kiss?"

He was finally starting to settle down. "Now how in the hell is that your business?"

"It's not," she said, flipping her hair back. "So…did you?"

"Yeah, we kissed. Happy?"

"Tongue?"

"Goddammit, Nikki."

"Okay," she said, laughing. "Okay."

"You guys are gonna get along great. You're just like her, stubborn as a mule. For weeks Rachel badgered me into going with her to Mill Creek until I finally gave in. It was a damn miracle Wallace never caught me sneaking off."

"What do you mean? Why would you have to sneak to go anywhere?"

Matt regretted his choice of words. Yeah, she already knew Wallace was the worst kind of father. On the other hand, it might help for her to see she hadn't missed out on anything. "He was strict. No after-school sports or any activities. I had to come right home and do chores around the ranch. No exceptions."

"That wasn't strict—it was mean." She leaned forward and squinted through the windshield at the upcoming signpost to Blackfoot Falls. He wondered if she realized they were about to turn off onto Lone Wolf land. "Could you have friends over?"

He grunted. "That would've been miserable and humiliating."

"Yeah, good point. What about Cole and Trace and the other brother? You guys were friends. Didn't you hang out?"

When he made the turn there was no mistaking they were close to the ranch. The air in the cab seemed to change. He could feel Nikki's tension swelling. Might've been his own.

It took him a minute to recall their conversation. "Nah, they were into sports and other things, which was just as well. Wallace doesn't like many people, but he outright hates the McAllisters."

"Why? They're so nice."

"Who knows? Jealousy, maybe. Until our generation came along the tension went back way before I was born." He'd unconsciously let up on the accelerator but it hadn't taken long to see lights. "You know where we are, right?"

"I know," she said softly. "I just don't know if I really want to meet him."

Since he couldn't fault her for that, he kept his mouth shut and drove. Low voltage security lighting seeped out from the stables and both barns. A few floodlights shined toward the corral and calving shed and several outbuildings scattered way in the back. The bunkhouse was ablaze with light. By now the hands were sucking down booze, playing cards and swapping stories they'd already told a dozen times.

And the old-timers were probably trying their damndest to figure out why the hell Matt Gunderson had come back.

The house itself was fairly dark. There was some light inside, a couple of lamps maybe, the timed night-lights that followed the stairs. But the porch, it was black.

And Wallace's SUV was nowhere to be seen.

The yellow-bellied prick had left.

"What's that?" Trace had entered the kitchen through the mudroom, sniffing the air and glancing around in search of the casserole Rachel had pulled out of the oven twenty minutes ago. "Smells like that cheesy chicken lasagna thing."

Right, except he wasn't getting his paws on it. "Why are you here and not helping corral the horses? It isn't even noon."

He frowned at the cooktop she'd just cleaned, opened one oven and then checked inside the other. "Where is it?"

Rachel shouldered him out of the way so she could get into the pantry. "It's not for you…therefore, you don't need to know."

He'd already pulled off his work gloves and stuffed them in his back jeans' pocket, and she knew darn well he'd try to filch a taste if he found it. "Boy, somebody's grouchy."

Not really, just in a hurry, but she could've been nicer. "Do you want lunch?"

"The casserole?" he asked, with a hopeful look.

"No." She sighed, accepting it was pointless to keep mum about her plan. "I made it for Nikki and Matt."

"They coming over?"

"I'm taking it to them."

"At the Lone Wolf?"

"Yes." She was prepared for him to call her crazy, but she'd never personally had a run-in with Mr. Gunderson.

"Why?"

"Why do you think? I'm being neighborly." Okay, there was more to the gesture. She wanted to see Matt again, but that was her own business.

"I should go with you. Give me a minute to change my shirt."

"No," she said, shaking her head when he opened his mouth to object. "I'm just dropping off the casserole. I don't need a bodyguard."

"I know." He raked a hand through his hair, shrugging. "I wouldn't mind seeing Matt again."

For being one of those effortlessly charming guys, Trace was a bad liar. Eyeing him, she pulled foil out of the drawer. "You're trying to weasel out of giving the new guests riding lessons."

"Wrong." He turned on the sink faucet to wash his hands. "For your information I already pawned that off on Josh."

"Thanks," she said with enough sarcasm to get his full attention. That he could look pleased with himself blew her mind. "I really need Cole in my face for pulling away one of his wranglers to entertain guests."

"He won't be upset. Don't get so jumpy." Frowning at her, Trace dried his hands. "Is it because of Matt?"

"Of course not." She busied herself with checking the semi-cooled casserole sitting under a dish towel on the kitchen table.

Trace stared at it and shook his head. "I know you had a crush on him back in the day...."

Her first impulse was denial. She paused. "You did not."

"Yep, we all did."

"Huh, really." She chuckled. "I thought I was being so sly. Anyway, that was a long time ago, and he's with Nikki now."

"They're just friends."

"Right." She'd spent an hour in bed last night analyzing Matt's assertion they weren't a couple. She believed him, yet there was a strong connection between them she couldn't put her finger on.

"He's not sleeping with her, if that's what's bothering you."

"Nothing is bothering me." She yanked a piece of foil from the roll a bit too enthusiastically. "How do you know he's not?"

"Can't explain it. I just do. If you asked Cole, he'd tell you the same thing."

"Jeez, I'm not asking Cole." She glanced toward the door to the dining room. Too late to worry about someone eavesdropping. "And don't you say anything." She exhaled. "About anything."

Grinning, Trace held up his hands. "Got it."

She felt a smile tug at her lips. He really was a good brother and a friend. When he wasn't being annoying. "I'll make another cheesy chicken casserole for you."

"Damn right you will."

"But I'm still going to the Lone Wolf by myself," she added, and noting his resigned nod, finally understood his motive for wanting to accompany her. "You want to see Nikki."

"I sure wouldn't mind." He reached into the ceramic cookie jar and stuck a chocolate chip cookie in his mouth while he pulled on a glove.

Nice trick. Rachel would have to remember that the next time she wanted to end a conversation. Though she was quite willing to let the matter drop. Too many thoughts about Matt were spinning inside her head. Their short time alone in the kitchen last night had proven they still had chemistry. If Nikki wasn't an obstacle, Rachel had to seriously consider how she should respond to the renewed attraction.

This wasn't Dallas. Having more than a twenty-minute public conversation with Matt would be enough to grease the Blackfoot Falls rumor mill. Then there was her 24/7 responsibility for the Sundance guests. That alone restricted her personal activities.

If she decided to go for it, but wasn't careful, she might as well take out an ad in the *Salina Gazette* that she wanted to sleep with Matt Gunderson.

THE GUNDERSON HOUSE remained well kept though not as pristine as she remembered. But since the economy had tanked, that was true of most of the ranches, including the Sundance. And yet the beige trim around the windows looked as if the paint had been touched up last summer and the shutters might've recently been replaced. The red door was the only thing different from ten years ago. After Matt had left, she hadn't come near the Lone Wolf.

She parked her mom's compact alongside Matt's truck under

the bare elm on the side of the house. Wallace's Escalade was nowhere in sight but that didn't mean he wasn't home. The SUV was new and pricey, and he might've parked it in one of the storage buildings around the property. Or maybe someone else had taken it out. She'd heard in town that he rarely drove anymore and when he did go out one of his guys accompanied him.

As much as she disliked the man, she still felt bad about his circumstances. He'd lost his wife three years ago, and that had to be hard on him. After her father had succumbed to cancer the whole family had suffered, but Rachel remembered too well how long it had taken her mom to rejoin the living.

She climbed out and went around to the passenger side to get the casserole. Two men working with a black stallion in the corral lifted their hands in greeting. She didn't recognize either of them, but she waved back, thinking how she'd known practically everyone when she was a kid. But going off to college had changed many things, most of them for the better, though some adjustments weren't coming so easily.

Snow that had been shoveled off the stone walkway and pushed to the side flanked her steps to the front door. The area was fairly clear, even in the shade, because there hadn't been a significant snowfall in a couple of weeks. It'd been a very weird winter, yet the weather hadn't hurt reservations at the Sundance. The guests kept coming, and if it weren't for Jamie's help, Rachel would have no life at all.

Standing at the door, balancing the casserole in one arm, she fluffed out the sides of her hair, then cleared her throat while she used the brass knocker.

Within seconds, Matt opened the door.

He wore jeans and an unbuttoned black shirt. The moment he saw her a smile curved his mouth.

"Hi." She tried so hard not to look at his chest.

"Come in." He stepped back, holding the door open wide.

She scraped off her boots, glancing around the foyer and

up the staircase as she crossed the threshold. "I can only stay a minute."

"Nikki's in her room and Wallace hasn't come home since last night." Matt closed the door. "I just made coffee. You want some?"

"Um, sure, if it's no trouble." Her gaze went to the strip of smooth skin where his shirt hung open.

"Sorry. I just got out of the shower," he murmured, glancing down, as if suddenly aware of his semi-clothed state.

"Here," she said, pushing the covered casserole at him, even though his fingers had gone to the first button.

Forced to abandon it, he accepted the dish. "What's this?"

"Dinner. Or lunch. Whatever. I made it this morning." She purposely avoided looking below his chin. Vaguely she realized he'd shaved. He looked more like her old Matt. Not his chest, though. Wow. "You'll just have to heat it."

"Thanks. Take off your jacket and come to the kitchen."

She started to shuck off the bulky down number while following him so he wouldn't have a chance to button up before she got another look. Yes, she was acting like a twelve-year-old. But it was February, and when would she likely see his naked chest again?

Of course there was a gigantically obvious answer. One that had her blushing by the time he set the casserole on the stainless steel stove and turned to look at her.

She pretended her arm was caught in the sleeve and twisted away to free herself.

"Need help?"

"I think I have it."

Ignoring her, he came around and easily slipped the jacket away from her body. If he knew she'd been faking, trying to cover her embarrassment, he didn't let on. He simply tossed the jacket on a kitchen chair, then brought his attention back to her, running his gaze down the front of the simple green turtleneck she'd tucked into her jeans.

"Nice job of filling out," he said, grinning as he leaned back, either for a better look or to duck a slap.

Rachel relaxed and eyed his chest. "I was thinking the same thing about you." This time she checked him out without a qualm, and noticed two scars that started between his rib cage, angling down until they disappeared behind the shirt.

Apparently they made him self-conscious. He pulled the front of his shirt together and started buttoning. "Yeah, I've been beat up some. Damn bulls...ornery sons of bitches." He gave her a crooked smile. "I need a new job."

Strange thing for him to say, even if he were joking. According to Trace, Matt was at the top of the heap and bull riders were a different breed of cowboy. They rode until they couldn't. "You're okay though, right?"

"Oh, yeah, it's nothing. Just ugly."

"I didn't mean the scars." She touched his hand, and he froze, leaving the last two buttons unfastened. "Which aren't ugly." She traced one of the marks with her thumb, only the part that was exposed, feeling him recoil, seeing the ridges of muscle in his belly tense.

"Rachel," he murmured, his voice a low uneven rasp. "What are you doing?"

She wondered how far the scar went, but she didn't dare reach inside his shirt. Fighting an urge to soothe the marred flesh with kisses, she lifted her gaze to his. "Tell me the truth, Matthew, are you all right?"

"Yes, I swear."

Neither of them looked away. "Isn't the Houston rodeo in February or March?" she asked, and finally remembered to lower her hand. She didn't want to—his skin was warm and smooth.... And she could smell the pine soap he'd used. "Trace said you've done well there for five consecutive years."

"What's your point?" He seemed tense, and she regretted being responsible.

"Why are you here and not there?"

Matt moved back and finished buttoning his shirt. "I can't make you believe me. But I'm fine. I only pulled out because I have business here. I'm still riding in the Houston Livestock Show and Rodeo later. It's a benefit for kids."

"I do believe you. I do…it's just that…" She sighed. "I looked you up on Google this morning. There's a ton of stuff about you online. I couldn't even make a dent—"

Exhaling loudly, he moved to the sophisticated silver coffee station that seemed out of place.

"What? It's not as if I read your diary."

A black mug already sat on the counter, and he took out another one from an upper oak cabinet. "Google, Yahoo, Twitter, all of that stuff boggles my mind. I'm happy just to make sense of my smartphone."

"It's huge and time-consuming, I'll admit. But I love social networking."

"Not me. I'm a simple cowboy." He poured her coffee, then got cream out of the fridge. "Either I win or lose—why anyone would care about all the other crap, I don't understand."

She'd read a few blogs about his early career he probably would rather see disappear, but nothing really awful so far. Now his reaction made her more curious. She could ask him…. No, the set of his jaw made it clear that might not go well.

Instead she spooned sugar from the canister into her coffee. "What kills me is that the whole time I was in school you were riding in rodeos all around Dallas and I didn't know."

His hand stilled. He didn't look up but seemed undecided whether or not to pour cream in his mug. "Would you have come to see me?"

"Of course I would have."

Matt set down the cream. He turned around, leaned back

against the blue-pearl granite counter and locked his gaze with hers. "Really?" he asked quietly. "Even after the way I left you?"

6

RACHEL STARED BACK AT HIM. She seemed to be giving the question serious thought, which he appreciated. "Yes," she said finally. "I would've gone to see you ride."

He wished she'd been more plain. Watching him ride wasn't the same as letting him know she was in the audience, or making an attempt to get in touch with him. He could ask. But damn, she'd been careful with her answer and that might be all he would get. It was probably more than he deserved.

She smiled. "It sure would've pissed me off if I couldn't get past those buckle bunnies throwing you their panties and phone numbers."

"Those women are nuts," he muttered, and turned back to fix his coffee. Had he already dumped in sugar or not?

"Are you blushing?" Rachel pulled his arm so he'd look at her.

"No."

"Yes, you are." She laughed, then squeezed his biceps. "Whoa, you filled out there, too."

He'd automatically flexed. "Try staying on a two-thousand-pound bull whose mission is to buck you off and pulverize you."

"Shoot, I missed my calling." She refused to move her hand, and as much as he liked her touching him, liked her standing so close he could see the tiny gold flecks of humor in her green eyes, in a few seconds it was gonna be awkward.

She smelled as sweet as honeysuckle and her lips were the color of ripe summer berries. And this was the second time since she'd taken off her jacket that she was making him hard. Hard enough that if she glanced down she wouldn't miss his cock bucking his fly.

"I'm sorry," she said, her hand trailing away with a reluctance that did nothing to settle him down. "I didn't mean to embarrass you, but I think it's adorable that you can still blush after all the female attention you get."

He moved back, held up his hands, as if he had nothing to hide. "I'm not embarrassed."

She blinked, and though she never actually looked at his fly, he knew the exact moment she became aware of his arousal. Her lips parted slightly, her lashes fluttered, and it seemed to take every bit of her willpower to keep her gaze on his face.

"Um, yeah. Okay." Color climbed her neck and filled her cheeks. "How about this warm weather we're having?" she said, unable to finish without laughing. "You're a horrible person."

Matt smiled. "A second ago I was adorable."

"I lied."

Catching her wrist, he stopped her from moving away and cupped her warm cheek. "You saw the best in me, Rachel. Always. No matter what anyone else said."

"I missed you so much," she whispered. "You broke my heart." Instantly, regret entered her eyes, and he could see she wanted to call back the words.

Selfishly he wished she could. He hadn't known for sure how she'd reacted to his leaving, but he'd made up great excuses in his head. "You were still young," he said, offering up his favorite. It was also true, but he'd left without facing her and that act of cowardice still nagged at him.

"I was." She shrugged and broke away to pick up her coffee.

"Sweet sixteen, a time for puppy love and broken hearts. Back then, anyway. Nowadays? Seems sixteen is the new thirty."

"Times and women have changed, that is for damn sure."

"You say that like it's a bad thing." Her lips were curved in the impish smile that once meant he'd end up tongue-tied, privately cursing himself for being a fool.

She'd always loved teasing him, and yeah, when he was a teenager she'd made him blush, which had royally pissed him off. But he'd been powerless to keep away from her. She had the kind of personality, the charismatic pull that drew people in. Her generous spirit made them want to stay. It wouldn't surprise him if it was Rachel who'd left a string of broken hearts.

He picked up his coffee and gestured at the kitchen table. They needed to sit down, at least he did. His body was finally getting a clue that he and Rachel weren't headed to happy hour. Didn't mean he was willing to test his cock's sketchy memory.

Taking her mug with her, she was first to sit, which allowed him to choose the chair across from her. Their knees might touch but that wouldn't get him in trouble. The sudden confusion on her face? Different story. Yeah, maybe he owed her more of an explanation, but this wasn't the time. Not with Nikki upstairs and Wallace likely to show up at any minute.

Rachel sipped from the mug, watching him over the rim, her eyebrows puckered in thought. "I should go," she said finally, and pushed back from the table. "This isn't a good time."

"For you?"

"No, for you." She paused. "You haven't seen your father yet, and when you do I doubt you want an audience."

"I saw him," Matt said, the image of Wallace passed out on the couch still sharp in his mind.

"Oh, last night you said…" She shook her head, looking confused. "Doesn't matter. I must've misunderstood."

"Technically, I saw him. But we haven't spoken. He was drunk when I got here. On his office couch, dead to the world."

She studied him for a moment, then let her gaze drop to her coffee. "I'm sorry. That had to be disappointing."

"Nope. Expected. The upside is that Nikki had a chance to get settled in peace."

The curiosity was back in Rachel's eyes, and he regretted mentioning Nikki. Whether she met Wallace today or not, he'd decided to talk to her about letting him explain their relationship to Rachel. Now that she'd met the McAllisters, he hoped she'd be cool with it.

"Look, I hope I'm not speaking out of turn," Rachel said, lowering her voice. "But if things get uncomfortable, we have room for you and Nikki at the Sundance."

"Thanks. I appreciate it, but I don't see us sticking around that long."

"No." Disappointment clouded her face. "I hate that."

"Why?" He gave her a neutral smile, tried to sound nonchalant, even though her frank reaction turned his heart into a jackhammer.

"You have to ask why?" She glared at him. "It's nice seeing you again, knowing you're okay, knowing that you haven't gotten too big for your britches."

A laugh escaped him. "What's that supposed to mean?"

"Oh, please, you know exactly what I'm talking about. Trace said you have the second-best bull riding record in the country."

"Nice of Trace to be keeping track of my career."

She sniffed. "I never followed rodeo so I didn't know—"

"That wasn't a jab. I meant it sincerely." He shrugged. "I like your brothers. I wish I'd known them better when I was younger."

"I know." She smiled sadly. "Your father, he doesn't have many fans but—"

"Don't worry about him," Matt cut in, hearing the bitter edge to his own voice. "He knows how to buy loyalty."

The sympathy in Rachel's eyes pissed him off almost as

much as his own careless slip. No, it wasn't a slip. Wrong word, because he didn't care. He felt no love or hate for Wallace; he felt nothing but indifference. And he doubted Wallace remembered he had a son. It seemed a convenient habit for the man to forget he had offspring.

"Look." Rachel reached across the table to cup her hand over the fist he'd made without realizing. "Obviously I know about your father's drinking problem. But he's been looking ill, and whether it's a result of the booze or not, I just want to say I think it's admirable that you've put your differences aside to come see him. That's all." Her hand trailed away as she leaned back. "I won't bring up the subject again."

Matt relaxed his fist. Her touch had calmed him some. He'd wondered how much she knew, what her mother might've told her. It was clear now that Rachel was in the dark, just as most people were in Blackfoot Falls, he suspected.

His coming home had nothing to do with caring about his father, and Rachel would see that soon enough. Maybe he should give a shit that she might not think so highly of him. And yeah, he did a little, but Rachel had never judged him. As a teenager she'd hotly and privately defended him against Wallace's injustices. Yet she'd never criticized him for not standing up to the man.

For his mother's sake, he'd forced himself to keep his cool, even when he'd started busting the seams of his clothes and was big enough to take the old man. Flatten him in the dirt. Keep him prone until he begged for mercy, until he apologized for every harsh word he'd uttered to his wife, every condemning glance he'd sent her, every second he'd made her weep in despair.

Yep, Matt could've humbled the bastard. But he'd swallowed his pride and his temper, held himself in check, until his self-control had started to slip. If he hadn't left, blood would've been shed. Wallace's blood. And as much satisfaction as that would've given Matt, it would have only added to his mother's misery. He never could've forgiven himself for that.

Rachel noisily cleared her throat, snapping him out of his preoccupation. "Will you remember the temperature to heat the casserole or should I write it down?"

"You're not leaving yet."

"I— You seem to have a lot on your mind."

"Yeah, sorry, it's weird being here," he said. "How about more coffee?"

She smiled. "My feelings won't be hurt if you want to be alone. I really get it."

"I want you to stay." He moved, intent on getting their coffee, and wincing when his chair scraped the wood floor.

"Wow, at my house that's punishable by a week of table clearing and washing dishes."

"Ouch. Your mother's tough."

"That's my rule."

He laughed. "I bet you have your brothers whipped into shape."

"If only…"

The rest of his coffee was cold so he dumped it in the sink. Rachel got up to help even though he motioned for her to stay seated. They didn't talk, just fixed each of their coffees, and then Rachel found a sponge and wiped down the counter.

If she'd wondered about his restraint back in the day, she never mentioned it. Never told him what he should do or pushed him into taking action. Pretty remarkable now that he thought about it. Not just because she herself had a spine of steel but because of her own experience. She'd had a perfect family until her father died when she was fourteen. Matt would bet his last dollar that Gavin McAllister had never abused his role as a father.

Everyone in the county liked and respected the man—how he did business, treated his neighbors and loved his family.

He'd produced another fine generation of McAllisters, a strong daughter and exemplary sons. People had said so, over and over again, without being asked as they stepped up to his casket. Even the old-timers hadn't been able to keep their eyes dry.

Two men couldn't be more different than Wallace Gunderson and Gavin McAllister. Matt never heard talk, but he knew what people thought. No one would go to Wallace's funeral. Well, Lucy would. As their housekeeper she'd seen plenty, but she was still loyal.

Either she was bucking for sainthood or, more likely, her diligence was his mother's doing. The woman could make a person promise things they regretted a moment later. Too bad Catherine Gunderson hadn't been able to work her magic on her husband.

Out of guilt, Matt rinsed the sink, and even used the spray nozzle since Rachel seemed determined to clean the countertop to death.

He sat down first so she would quit fussing and join him. "How long you plan on staying at the Sundance?"

Her back was to him and he couldn't see her face, but the way she stiffened had him examining his own question. "Why?" she asked, squeezing out the sponge, then tucking it behind the spigot before turning around. "That's an odd question. Except for college, I've lived there all my life."

"Yeah." He waited until she sat again. "So? Going to college, getting a degree, that had to change your outlook."

She opened her mouth to say something, then pressed her lips together and shook her head.

Obviously it was a loaded question, but he hadn't meant to put her on the spot. "You seem happy. I don't know why I asked."

"I have a responsibility to keep the dude ranch profitable and running smoothly, at least for now."

He knew last night that her being here had something to do

with helping her family. She'd slithered out of an explanation, calling it complicated, but he knew Rachel. She was doing what she always did—she was taking the bull by the horns, finding solutions, making things work, even if it meant shelving her own dreams for a while. He didn't fault her for delaying her future to help her family. Her selfless nature was one of the many things about her he admired.

"And later?" he asked. "What are you looking at doing down the road?"

"Hotel management. That's what I have a degree in." Her lips pulled into a wry smile. "Ironic, huh? I end up running a dude ranch."

"Good practice."

"Funny." She slumped back. "My mom and brothers have no idea how I feel, so you can't say anything."

"They won't hear it from me." He sipped his coffee, bothered that she didn't feel she could freely confide in them. "You might decide you aren't cut out for dealing with guests. I've stayed in my share of hotels, and I've seen the staff jump through hoops trying to please guests. It's kind of sickening."

"That's just part of the biz."

"Maybe so, but I know that temper of yours."

She glared, her lips parted, and then let out a huffing snort that made him laugh. She crumpled a paper napkin from the silver holder and threw it at him.

He caught it midchest. "You see what I mean?"

"I can behave like an adult when I need to. Apparently you bring out the worst in me."

"You can't blame me for that purple hair. I wasn't even here."

"What?" She was trying to stare him down and not laugh. "For your information, this is very stylish."

"Is that a fact?"

"Yes, it is."

"You wouldn't have trouble getting a hotel manager's job looking like that?"

"Well, I'm not looking for one right now, am I?"

"I reckon family-owned dude ranches aren't so picky."

The fire disappeared from her eyes and she seemed to deflate right in front of him. "No," she said. "So there is that upside."

"Hey." He reached across the table for her hand. "You know I'm just teasing."

Her lips twitched into a smile, though not the one he was hoping for. He'd unintentionally hit a nerve. "You sure had me fooled. I used to think you were such a sweet boy."

"Sweet?" He spit it out like a cussword. "You have me mixed up with someone else." He picked up her hand and turned it over so that their palms met. "When do you figure you'll get the Sundance back on its feet?"

"When beef prices stabilize and the cost of corn stops climbing."

"In other words, you have no idea."

"Sadly, none."

"I'm sorry," he said, treading carefully, wondering how he could pitch in. "You guys don't deserve this. Your family was always the first to lend a hand to any rancher down on his luck."

"Everyone is struggling and none of them deserve it." She sighed. "I think what kills Cole the most is that men he's known his whole life have asked for work and he's had to turn them down. He's been running the Sundance on fumes to avoid layoffs."

Matt stared at their joined hands. How could he offer to help without ruffling feathers? He had money, a lot of it. What a guy his age with a basic education could make riding a bull was almost obscene. In the beginning when he'd started earning big, he'd done his share of reckless spending. Fast cars, gorgeous women, and shelling out cash to just about anyone with a heartbreaking story and their hand out.

It was one of the rodeo clowns who'd set him straight. The old-timer had warned him to quit being a dumb-ass and think about his future so he wouldn't end up pushing sixty and running around the arena in a costume distracting bulls. Matt had taken heed, even though it was for the wrong reason. He'd wanted to show up Wallace.

Rachel moved her hand, and he looked up into her eyes. They were so beautiful, a true green, the color of spring grass that April showers help spread over the hills behind the Lone Wolf. How many times had he chased her up there, headed for Mill Creek, knowing each time he was asking for trouble? God, he'd wanted her with a fierceness that burned low in his belly and kept him awake too many nights.

"You're so quiet," she said, her gaze roaming his face. "What are you thinking about?"

He smiled. "Don't believe you wanna know."

Her brows arched slightly. "I might surprise you." She gave him a sexy dare-you look that reminded him she wasn't that off-limits kid anymore. "Tell me."

"I will." He released her hand. "If you come over here."

She frowned as if trying to figure out what he was up to, then smiled when he pushed back his chair. "This better be good if you're making me get up."

"I doubt you'll complain."

Rachel let out a short laugh. "Seems you've gotten a bit cocky, Matthew Gunderson."

"Yes, ma'am, I reckon I have."

"Oh, and laying it on thick, too."

He leaned back, tracking her as she moved around the table, her fingers grazing the oak surface as she took her time, her gaze refusing to break from his. "I'll try to mind my manners," he said and willed his body to calm down.

"No, don't do that." Her mouth lifted in a teasing grin, and he really liked that she still blushed.

A second before she moved within reach, the dogs started barking. She froze and turned her head toward the window.

"It's nothing," Matt said, knowing the pair of border collies belonged to the hands who lived in the bunkhouse.

"They weren't here earlier." She stepped away from him. "Your father might be home."

"Rachel, wait." Matt jumped to his feet.

He couldn't guarantee the barking meant nothing, but that wouldn't stop him. He caught her hand and pulled her close. Startled, she lifted her eyes to his face, her lips parted.

Her skin looked so soft he had to touch her cheek. It felt like silk under the pad of his thumb. No one had skin this satiny, only Rachel.

He lowered his head, and she raised hers. Their lips met, and his heart nearly exploded because he'd spent half the night picturing this moment. She placed her hands on his shoulders, and he drew her into his arms, pulling her closer. Her fingers slowly curled into his muscles, and he slanted his mouth over hers.

She tasted so sweet, her mouth soft, yielding and familiar even after all the years. But when he slid his tongue between her lips, there was nothing familiar in the way she welcomed him to delve and explore. Rachel was all woman now, stoking the heat that had been simmering inside him since he'd seen her last night.

He slid a hand down her spine, wanting to touch every inch of her. Her breasts felt full and heavy crushed to his chest, and damn, he wished they were just about anywhere but the kitchen. Her hands slipped over his shoulders up the back of his neck until her fingers combed through his hair....

Abruptly she broke away. "Matt," she said, breathlessly. "The dogs—" Her face flushed, her eyes unfocused, she blinked blearily at him. "They're still barking."

"The hell with them." He pulled her back in and pressed his mouth against hers.

She gave in, started to kiss him, but then jerked away, shaking her head. "No. I have to go."

He had no choice but to release her. She'd tensed, the mood was broken. A curse slipped out that he hadn't intended. "Sorry."

"I know," she said, smiling. "You have a pen?"

He wasn't thinking too clearly, but he remembered one had always sat by the kitchen phone.

She grabbed the small notepad along with the ballpoint and scribbled something. "My number," she said, passing it to him. "Call whenever." And she was gone without looking back.

7

RACHEL WAS RIGHT. The dogs had been barking at a truck that had turned onto the driveway. It wasn't Wallace, but one of the cowboys who lived in the bunkhouse. She'd left anyway, and Matt knew it was for the best. Wallace had to come home sometime, and there was Nikki to consider. Matt still didn't like it. Man, he'd just started getting warmed up. They had a lot more talking and kissing to do, and he hoped there'd be less clothes and more skin down the road.

Evidently he'd underestimated the level of anxiety that had been dogging him over how he'd left Rachel. Now that he knew she hadn't written him off or branded him a coward, he felt lighthearted, optimistic. No other way to describe the ease in his chest or explain the fact he could look around the place without the memories strangling him like a bolo tie he'd pulled too tight.

Half an hour after she left, he looked out the window and saw Petey walking from the corral to the barn. The wrangler had been with the Lone Wolf for as long as Matt could remember. The giant of a man had always been gruff and rarely cracked a smile. Come to think of it, with all the wiry hair on his head and face, a smile could get lost. Chuckling at the thought, Matt grabbed his jacket off the oak coat tree on his way to the front door.

As a kid he'd stayed clear of Petey. Matt had heard whispers about Petey wrestling bears or being able to kill a man with his bare hands. Now he knew the men had been poking fun at him, but at the time no one could've convinced him that the huge utility knife clipped to Petey's belt was only used for shaving and camping.

After leaving Blackfoot Falls, Matt hadn't given the guy a thought—until his mother's funeral. Petey had cleaned up, even wore an old brown suit to the church and sat in the second row, behind the family, while all the other hands gathered in the back. Matt almost hadn't recognized him without his beard. But Petey had tapped him on the shoulder, leaned over, his pale eyes filled with tears and told Matt how sorry he was because Catherine Gunderson had been a fine lady.

Sitting behind Matt, Wallace had stared stoically at the flower-draped casket. Until that moment, Matt figured it wasn't possible to hate his father more. Turned out he'd underestimated himself.

But hatred eventually made a man weak and reckless. And Matt was glad he'd learned that lesson early, before he'd gotten himself killed by a bull or knifed in a bar fight. He'd been lucky. Damn lucky.

Matt's boots crunched the gravel and snow as he skirted a pair of four-wheelers that shouldn't have been left in the middle of the turnaround. "Hey, Petey."

The man had disappeared into the barn, but ducked back outside, tugging down the brim of his battered hat and squinting into the sunlight. "Is that you, kid?"

"Depends which kid you mean."

His beard moved and there was a brief flash of off-white teeth. Son of a gun…it was a smile. "The smart-ass one," Petey grumbled while removing a work glove.

Matt grinned. "Yeah, that's me," he said, accepting the man's extended hand, which was the size of a small ham. After a couple of hearty pumps, Matt winced. "Jesus, I still need this."

"Come on, big rodeo star like you." Petey squeezed tighter, just enough to make Matt cuss but not cry. "You don't want people thinking you shake like a girl."

Matt snorted. "Seriously, I have to be able to hold a rope, or you're gonna be coming to *my* funeral."

Petey released him, and Matt drew back, flexing his hand and glancing around to see if the men were having a laugh.

And then he realized what he'd said, and shot a look at Petey. A sick feeling burned in Matt's gut at the memory of his mom's casket being lowered into the ground…of the tears in the big man's eyes…the lack in Wallace's.

"You're right." He clapped Matt's shoulder. "I shouldn't be horsing around. But you got a mean grip yourself there, kid." Petey did some hand-flexing of his own, then shook his head with amusement. "Holding on to a ton of bull flesh, guess you gotta be strong or get dead."

"Yep," Matt agreed. "I try real hard not to get dead."

Laughing, Petey yanked his hat off to scratch his head. His hair had thinned—what was left was as gray as it was black. "I never figured you for a bull rider."

Matt had heard the same thing from reporters. Riding was often a family tradition, the lifestyle passed down to boys who started the sport young. "I got that ornery Gunderson blood in me. I reckon that makes me and the bull pretty even."

"You got your ma's fine blood in you, too," Petey said quietly. "Don't you forget that."

"No, sir. Keeps me sane."

"Before you got famous your ma used to tell me you were riding broncs."

After the funeral, Matt had wondered about his mom and

Petey's relationship. He hadn't asked then, wouldn't ask now. "I didn't want her worrying."

"I figured as much." Petey resettled his hat on his head. "She did anyway. I reckon that's what ma's do. But she was proud of you, too. Whether you took first place or not."

"After I took the world finals and all the publicity started, there was no more hiding the truth. And man, did I get an earful. No congratulations or asking what I was gonna do with all the money I'd won. She only asked if I had any idea how dangerous bull riding was." Matt smiled. "'Course I failed to mention I'd cracked two ribs that night."

Petey laughed. "She tracked down every article on you she could find. They'd be goin' on about your perfect form, or how you broke records and the part she'd read out loud was when you said, 'yes, sir' and 'no, sir.'" Petey looked off toward the snow-packed mountains. "She'd get that pretty smile on her face, proud that she raised you right."

"She did." Matt swallowed around a lump in his throat. "I'm glad you were here for her."

He tugged down the brim of his hat. "Ah, we all miss her."

That was a lie, Matt thought, his gaze wandering toward the house, though one better left alone. This visit was about Nikki. Losing sight of that fact could kick up dust and blur a man's vision. "You know where Wallace is?"

Petey snorted, shaking his head. "We don't talk much. Never have."

"Just as well."

"You seen him yet?"

"Nope. He was passed out drunk when I arrived the first time. Then gone when I came back."

Petey stroked his scraggly beard. "Might be more than the booze knocking him down. I expect Lucy probably knows something." He eyed Matt. "You here on account he's ailing or because you got hitched?"

"No, I'm not married and I don't give a shit if he is sick. Whatever's kicking his ass he brought on himself. How often does Lucy come by?"

"Two or three times a week. She cooks meals, makes sure he eats. Not like those two hotheads he keeps around."

"Who?"

"You'll meet 'em." Petey grunted. "Tony ain't so bad— it's the other one…he's got the temper. No neck, built like a Brahma, the kid's got more muscles than brains."

That didn't sound like the kind of men Wallace would hire. "They from around here?"

"Nah, nobody knows those two. He hired 'em a few months back. They aren't social. You might catch one or the other at the Watering Hole, but mostly they don't leave Wallace's side."

Matt started to ask something when the collies came bounding out of nowhere, their loud barks drowning him out.

Petey motioned toward the truck or Wallace's large SUV, hard to tell, speeding down the gravel driveway too fast. Whoever was at the wheel was an idiot. Which could easily mean Wallace, though for all his faults, he'd never been a reckless driver. Maybe long-term boozing had changed that.

"Reckon I'll be getting back to work." Petey pulled on his glove. "Sure good to see you, kid."

"Who is that? Wallace?"

"Tony or the hothead. Your pa don't hardly drive no more, but likely he's with 'em or they'd have their own truck. Don't let him get you riled," Petey said, then headed inside the barn.

Matt watched the vehicle approach. He considered giving Nikki a heads-up, but he didn't feel like having an audience when he saw Wallace. He didn't care about the two guys babysitting him. As long as they weren't giving the hands a hard time, Matt had no call to make them his business.

At the last minute, he turned and headed for the house. They would've seen him. He hoped that didn't mean they'd turn around or Wallace would refuse to come inside. Nikki's nerves were on edge and she wouldn't agree to stick around much longer. The idea would bother him less if he hadn't seen Rachel again.

Those sparkling eyes, that fiery hair and generous smile. What a beauty. And smart, too, with a heart as big as the whole state of Montana. She'd seen his pain, his despair, his frustration and she'd never run from him, never done anything but accept him. Even though she probably hated the Gunderson name as much as everyone else in her family...hell, maybe the entire county....

Matt had to get this matter with Nikki squared away, free himself to spend time with Rachel. He went in through the front door and straight to the window to watch the SUV pull under the covered space near the stables where it had been parked yesterday.

Goddamn Wallace, if he didn't get inside right now, Matt would drag him in. He would...

The driver's door opened, and Petey was right, the guy who climbed out was all muscle and no neck. He had a mean squinty stare that he aimed at the house. When the other two doors opened, Matt knew Wallace was there.

"Hey."

He turned when he heard Nikki, standing at the top of the stairs, hands stuffed in her jeans, her shoulders hunched as if she were cold. "You okay?" he asked, pulling off his jacket.

"I heard the dogs barking? Is it him?"

"I think so. Wait in your room until I call you, if you want. Or not."

She bit at her lower lip. "Yeah, let's stick with the plan." She hesitated. "Let me know if it's not him."

"You got it." He watched her slip down the hall, then he turned back to the window.

The SUV had already been abandoned. He couldn't see anyone, had no way to tell which direction everyone had gone. If Wallace planned on coming inside, it had to be through the kitchen or Matt would see him out front.

He hung his jacket on the hall coat tree, listening until he heard the back door open and close. No voices, so that was good. Drawing in a deep breath, he moved into the den and made himself comfortable on the red leather chair that matched the couch. It wouldn't matter if Wallace planned on hiding in his office, took the stairs or went into the living room. From Matt's vantage point, he'd see him.

After rattling around the kitchen for a few minutes, Wallace walked into the den. He slid a glance at Matt, but didn't miss a step on his way to the wet bar at the back of the room. He took a glass off the shelf and grabbed a bottle of Jim Beam. After he poured a couple of fingers worth, he hesitated, then brought down a second glass.

"Your woman make the food sitting in the kitchen?" he asked, his back to Matt as he poured again.

Matt didn't answer, just watched in pure amazement. This was all the man had to say after not seeing his son in the three years since his wife's funeral. But then, no reason to be surprised, they hadn't said a word to each other after the service. Matt had grabbed his bag and left.

"You drunk?" Matt asked, studying him closely. He seemed coordinated enough and hadn't slurred his words.

"Not yet." Wallace carried both glasses from the bar, his pallor and frail body as startling to Matt today as it was yesterday. "You come to help build my coffin?" Wallace asked, his bloodless lips curled in a faint sneer as he passed the whiskey to Matt.

"I've never been good with a hammer," he said, "but I'm willing to give it a shot."

Wallace chuckled. "There's hope for you yet, boy." He raised his glass in salute, then downed the liquor.

Matt gritted his teeth, watching Wallace go back for the bottle. "Can you lay off the booze for a while? I want you to meet someone."

He slowly put the whiskey down, kept his back to Matt and stared at the wall where a mirror had once been part of the intricately hand-carved bar. The frame was still a beautiful piece, made from mesquite brought from Texas, a one-of-a-kind beveled mirror from New Orleans and crafted by Matt's great-great-grandfather. The meticulous work had stretched over two winters and got passed down through three genera- tions. In a drunken rage, it took Wallace only seconds to smash the glass and ruin the family heirloom forever.

Matt had just turned twelve. His mother had cried for an hour, and he'd felt guilty because it was the one time he hadn't blamed Wallace. The bastard probably hated looking himself in the eye, and try as he might, Matt couldn't fault him for that.

After a long tension-charged moment, Wallace turned around, no glass, no bottle in his hands. He looked confused, his features pinched as he reached behind and held on to the bar as if to steady himself. "You actually *want* me to meet her?"

Matt finally understood, and he almost laughed. "Yeah, I came home for your blessing."

The second Wallace recognized Matt's sarcasm, he clenched his jaw. "Where is she?"

"Upstairs."

"Better get moving before I change my mind about that drink."

"Why don't you sit down?" Matt got to his feet and noticed how heavily Wallace sagged against the bar.

"I don't need you ordering me around."

He shook his head, not just at Wallace's scowl but at Matt's own foolishness. Poking the man into a foul mood right be- fore he met Nikki was plain stupid. Matt stopped at the foyer. "How've you been?"

"Shitty."

"Anything I should know about?"

Wallace hesitated, then cursed. "Lucy?"

"What about her?"

"She wrote you."

"Nope, and I haven't seen her since Mom's funeral."

Wallace's gray eyebrows dipped into a suspicious frown. "Why are you really here?"

"Already told you. I want you to meet someone." Matt started for the stairs, then stopped long enough to add, "I'll tell you this, she's not my wife or my girlfriend."

With that he raced up the stairs. They had nothing more to say to each other, but Nikki and Wallace might have plenty. She must've heard him because she opened her door before he made it to the landing and stared at him with uncertainty.

"Ready?" he asked.

"No." She breathed in deeply, closed the door behind her and dragged her palms down the front of her jeans. "Where is he?"

"In the den."

"Drunk?"

"Not yet." Matt waited for her to join him on the stairs and then slid an arm around her shoulders. "You have the upper hand," he whispered. "You say whatever you want. I'm with you all the way."

"Thanks." She exhaled. "Go first."

He took his time, then waited at the bottom, his heart twisting with each slow painful step she took. When she motioned for him to enter the den first, he took the lead, panicking for a second when he didn't spot Wallace. Then he saw him, sitting in the longhorn chair near the bar, small and frail, his hands clasped between his thin legs.

It was gonna take some doing for Matt to get used to the new image. His father had been a virile handsome man well into his fifties. Next to him on the side table was the Jim Beam bottle and the empty glass.

"Come on." Matt gestured for Nikki when he realized she was still at the bottom of the stairs.

She lifted her chin and moved to stand alongside Matt, her cynical gaze slowly finding the man who'd fathered her.

"This is Nikki," Matt said, switching his attention to Wallace's drawn face.

He stared, the prominent Adam's apple in his thin neck bobbing with a convulsive swallow. Leaning slightly forward, he blinked at her rapidly then squinted, as if struggling to focus. His lips moved, but nothing came out, and the desperation in his tortured eyes actually got to Matt.

"Wallace Gunderson," Nikki said, her voice flat. "You look nothing like your picture."

He slowly shook his head, as if in disbelief. And then the strangest damn smile pulled at the corners of his mouth. "Rosa," he whispered, and tried unsuccessfully to stand.

Nikki jerked.

Matt took hold of her arm. They'd come too far for her to run just because Wallace had mistaken her for her mother. Of course Matt hadn't seen this coming either. She resembled Rosa some, but not enough for his father to be confused. But then Matt hadn't seen her as a young woman. And Rosa had lived a hard life, largely thanks to Wallace.

He gave up trying to stand. Just sat there smiling, and whispering Rosa's name again.

"Wallace, this is Nikki. Not Rosa." Matt tried to urge her into the room but she wouldn't move.

She held up a finger, glaring at Wallace, her anger so potent it seemed to suck the air from the room. "You aren't allowed to say her name. Ever. You understand me?"

"But—" His shocked gaze darted to Matt. "Why?"

"Nikki is your daughter, Wallace. Yours and Rosa's."

She twisted away from Matt, her body tense and ready to bolt. "I can't do this."

"Wait." He sent her a pleading look. "Please, Nikki, for me."

"Don't, Matt." Her lashes fluttered, trying to stop the moisture from seeping down her cheeks. He'd only seen her cry once, even though she'd had plenty of reason for tears. "Damn you, Matt, don't ask this of me," she begged softly.

"I've only loved two women," Wallace said, drawing their attention back to him. "My whole life. I know it was wrong, but I loved them both so much that I..." His voice trailed off and he slumped back, his shoulders sagging in defeat, his chin dropped to his narrow chest.

Matt stared at him. Yeah, the old man admitted to loving Rosa. But it was the first time Matt had heard Wallace say he cared for Catherine Gunderson, the woman who'd loved him blindly and devoted her life to him. Not even at her funeral had he said the word. Yet he had loved her...in his own warped selfish way....

Something weird shifted inside Matt's chest.

"I'm sorry, Matt." Nikki had already backed into the foyer.

"Hey," he said, following her. "We knew this would be rough."

"It's stupid and hopeless, and I can't stay here." She grabbed the railing. "I have to go back to Houston."

"Let's take a minute. I'll come upstairs with you." He glanced back at Wallace, who'd found the energy to tip the bottle to his glass.

"Fine." Sniffing, she turned to find her footing on the first step. "You can watch me pack."

He stayed on her heels. "How about the Sundance? Would you feel comfortable staying there?"

She stopped halfway and cautiously met his eyes. "Just being in the same room with him makes me sick."

"I know." Matt scrubbed at his face. "I understand," he said, lying, because he was at a complete loss. He didn't know what the hell was going on in his brain. Nikki, Rachel, Wallace, his mother…everything was a damn jumble. "Give me…give this thing with Wallace a few more days?"

Nikki studied him, as if he'd spoken to her in a foreign language she had to translate. Her lips slowly curved in a worried smile. She hesitated, then rubbed his arm. "Sure, Matt. I can do that."

8

RACHEL'S DAY IMPROVED a hundred percent after she answered Matt's call. Hilda and her mother had offered to cover for her in the kitchen so she could ready Nikki's room. They probably suspected she was anxious to race upstairs to touch up her makeup before Matt arrived within the hour. Not that she cared. They knew about the casserole she'd taken to the Lone Wolf, and when she returned she might've been a bit flushed and chattered on about Matt a minute or two longer than prudent....

Oh, well, it seemed her teenage crush on him hadn't been the secret of the century she'd imagined. No big deal. And if her mom's and Hilda's shared glances meant they thought she might still have a crush on him, that didn't bother Rachel either.

That kiss.

The new hard body Matt was rocking.

And holy crap, that huge bulge behind his fly this morning... If her adrenaline hadn't been pumping before, it was now.

Reaching the top of the stairs, she sighed happily. Oh, they were so going to do more than kiss. Location could be a problem. Plus there was Nikki to consider. They couldn't ignore her. Trace would eagerly step in and keep her entertained, but Rachel wasn't sure if Nikki would like that. Ninety-five percent of the single women in the county would offer to have Trace's firstborn. Just Rachel's luck, Nikki hadn't been dazzled.

She slowed her pace, thinking that if she had a shred of decency she'd be more concerned about why their plans had changed. Why Nikki no longer wanted to stay at the Lone Wolf. Matt had sounded a little off during their brief conversation, but Rachel figured it was because he wasn't alone.

The downstairs grandfather clock chimed and got her moving again. She was putting Nikki on the same floor with the family. One room was still available in the guest wing, but only for a couple of days and then the Sundance would be booked for the rest of the week.

Passing her own room somehow reminded her that she hadn't shaved her legs in a week. Wow, remembering at the last second would've been awful. Though she was jumping the gun. Matt could simply drop off Nikki, and Rachel wouldn't see him again until they were ready to leave Blackfoot Falls.

No, she couldn't let that happen. Matt wouldn't let that happen, not after this morning. But he'd left before, without warning.

Just like that her mood plummeted. Logically she understood this time was different. They were both leaving eventually. He'd be going much sooner, but that didn't matter because she had no expectation he would stay. She opened the door to the room, relieved to see Hilda had already changed the sheets and dusted the oak dresser and matching nightstands.

Rachel had no idea how long she'd been standing there, her thoughts drifting back and forth to Matt, when she heard the doorbell. Quickly she grabbed towels from the linen closet and set them on the bed, then hurried down the hall despite knowing someone would beat her to the door.

Her mother was hugging a very somber Matt when Rachel started down the stairs. Nikki stood off to the side, her face pale and tense. Seeing her made Rachel feel like crap. Obviously something horrible had happened, most likely Wallace-related, while Rachel had been wrapped up dreaming of Matt.

"Hi, Nikki, I'm sorry I missed you earlier." Rachel stopped in front of her, hesitant yet longing to hug her because she seemed so small and lost.

"My fault. I was hiding in my room." Nikki managed a faint smile. "Not from you," she added quickly and drew in a shaky breath. "Thanks for putting me up. Really, I know y'all are busy. Do I pay now or when I leave?"

"Oh, my goodness, Nikki." Barbara McAllister had no qualms about ignoring boundaries. She pulled Nikki into a hug. "You're our guest. You and Matt are always welcome here."

Nikki turned to Matt for help. "But—"

He was staring at Rachel, his face grim enough to make Rachel's heart thud.

She broke eye contact first. "Forget it," she said to Nikki. "Mom's had practice arguing with four kids. She has final say."

Nikki moved back. "This isn't supposed to be charity," she murmured.

"It's not." Matt finally weighed in. "I'm paying for Nik's room."

"I can pay for my own," she said, and gave him a blistering look.

"Ah, Jesus." He plowed a hand through his hair, then winced. "Sorry, Mrs. McAllister."

She laughed. "Matthew, I have three sons."

Rachel tried to look innocent.

Her mom arched a brow at her. "And this one."

Nikki laughed a little at that.

Matt's mood hadn't lightened at all, and it broke Rachel's heart. The problem had to be Wallace. For Matt it had always been his bastard of a father. She had a good mind to jump in her car and go give him a dressing-down that was late in coming. He had this great son who'd defended him all his childhood, who'd broken his back to earn Wallace's approval, and the stupid idiot had never once…

"Rachel?"

She blinked at Matt. He was staring at her. So was everyone else.

"Rachel," her mom repeated gently. "Why don't you show Nikki to her room?"

"Sure," she muttered, heat climbing her neck. "Of course."

"Actually, if you have a few minutes, I'd like to talk to you," Matt said. "I mean everyone. You, too, Hilda, if you have time. I assume the guys are out working."

Rachel turned to see their housekeeper standing near the door between the dining room and kitchen. She'd been with them so long, she was practically family.

"Please, come." Rachel saw the embarrassment in the older woman's dark eyes, probably worried they thought she was eavesdropping, and motioned for her to join them.

Nikki glanced toward the back of the house, then toward the stairs. "We can't talk out here."

All the guests were gone, enjoying outdoor activities, but the foyer was airy and huge and it didn't matter that they were alone in the house. It could feel intimidating for a personal conversation.

"We can go to Cole's office," Rachel said. "Or have coffee in the kitchen. No one else is home. Jamie ran into town an hour ago. I don't know when she'll be back."

Matt glanced at Nikki, who nodded. "The kitchen is okay, and if Jamie shows up, that's fine."

They settled at the table in silence. Hilda seemed nervous. Rachel definitely had a jitter in her belly. Oddly, her mother didn't even seem curious, as if she already knew what Matt was going to say. Strange, really strange. She hadn't seen or talked to him last night, or since he'd arrived.

Matt had taken the chair next to Nikki, and with a fond

smile, reached over to squeeze her hand. Rachel had some nerve feeling jealous, but there it was.

"Nikki," he said, "is my sister."

"Half sister," she corrected, giving Rachel time to close her mouth.

His shoulders lifted in a slight shrug, and he looked at Rachel and Hilda. "No one else knows. Not Lucy or any of the Lone Wolf hands. Wallace just found out. We left him halfway into a bottle."

After an awkward silence, Rachel knew she should say something, but what? A few weird thoughts flitted through her head. Of course Nikki had to be Wallace's daughter, not Catherine's. She'd lived her whole adult life at the Lone Wolf. Everyone in Blackfoot Falls would have known if she'd had a second pregnancy. Besides, insane as it was, Catherine Gunderson had adored her husband. With a sinking feeling, Rachel wondered if she'd known of his infidelity.

She focused on Nikki. "If you don't mind my asking, did he know about you before today?"

The younger woman nodded, her lashes briefly lowering, then she tossed her hair in a gesture of defiance. "He did, not that it mattered."

Dammit, Rachel wished she'd kept her mouth shut. "I shouldn't have asked…. I'm not sure why I did…sorry…."

"It's okay." Nikki laughed nervously. "Y'all know him better than I do. He's a piece of…a jerk. Can't hide that in a town this small." She sighed, slanting a glance at Matt. "I want to leave. Matt doesn't. I have to calm down, and we'll see."

Rachel met his eyes, but quickly turned away, not wanting him to see the panic that rose in her throat and probably showed in her face. God, he couldn't leave so soon. They'd just reconnected.

"Would you like to stay with us, too, Matt?" her mom asked. "Everyone would love having you here." She leaned in, lowering her voice, a trace of amusement making the skin around her eyes crinkle. "Some of our paying guests can be somewhat persistent, but I think we can count on Rachel to keep the women away from you."

She glared at her mother, then out of the corner of her eye saw Nikki and Hilda fighting smiles. Rachel switched her gaze back to Matt. His serious expression had faded, the slight twitch of his lips unmistakable.

Oh, brother… "You better believe it," she said with a defeated laugh. "You are officially off-limits. I'll post signs."

"Thanks, but…" Matt slowly shook his head, mouth now tight. The light moment was gone, though he didn't seem the least embarrassed. Ten years ago his face would've been beetred. But he was a celebrity now, which Rachel kept forgetting, and a guy as hot as Matt could probably have his pick of women.

Was Rachel fooling herself that he was interested in her? Though he had kissed her first. And it would just be sex—they both understood that. The subject of forever after would never have to come up.

"Matt?" Nikki found his hand. "It would be fun to stay here. Please."

He didn't answer, but he wasn't going to stay. It was clear by the way he'd drawn back his shoulders. He was holding his ground. But why would he want to stay in the same house as Wallace? That was crazy.

"I'll think about it," he said finally.

"Well, that means no." Nikki sighed and shoved his hand away. Apparently she did know her brother. "Fine."

He tugged at her hair. "I'm still going to be around, so don't be a sourpuss."

Rachel smiled. They were cute together. She'd bet he actually enjoyed having a kid sister. "Nikki, the town's annual

Valentine's dance is day after tomorrow. If you don't have anything to wear, we'll find you something."

"They still have that dance?" Matt asked.

"It's Blackfoot Falls. Why would anything change?" Rachel regretted the sarcasm when she noticed her mom's disappointed frown. "It'll be fun."

"I don't dance," Matt muttered.

Nikki shook her head. "Me, neither."

"Tough. You guys are both coming. You can gorge on cupcakes and punch."

"Still bossy," Matt murmured, his gaze locked with hers.

"Yep." Rachel's heart skipped a couple of beats. The affectionate way he was looking at her, they could've been the only ones in the kitchen.

The sound of a distinctive engine from outside broke the brief spell.

"It's Jamie," Hilda said, and got up from the table. "She picked up groceries for me. I'll go help her." Matt immediately pushed back his chair, but Hilda waved him to stay seated. "It's one bag. Nikki, I'm very glad you'll be staying with us, *chica,*" she said with warmth and sincerity as she touched Nikki's shoulder.

She gave Hilda a grateful smile then watched her head outside. "Is she from here?"

"Hilda lives with us." Barbara shrugged. "She has for, gosh, I don't know, since before Rachel was born."

"Even before Trace. Isn't Ben about Jesse's age?" Rachel said to her mom, and then to Nikki, "She has a son and daughter. They moved here from Mexico with her. We grew up with them."

"Here? All of you?"

Rachel nodded. "It's a big house." She noticed Nikki's surprise, and that Matt seemed pleased. Of course he knew Hilda and her kids, so this wasn't news, which meant he wanted Nikki to hear this. What was he up to?

"Hilda's always been like everyone's grandmother," Matt said to his sister. "Remember when you asked me how I knew so many Spanish cusswords?"

"She did not teach you those," Barbara said, her eyes narrowing.

"Well, that sucks." Rachel snorted. "She didn't teach *me*."

"Hold on, ladies," Matt said, grinning. "You didn't let me finish. Ben was the one who rounded out my education and cussing seemed to be the only Spanish he knew. Where is he these days?"

Rachel and her mom both shook their heads, Barbara throwing a pointed glance at the back door.

Matt gave a small nod, and dropped the subject. "I'll take your bag upstairs for you, Nik, then I have to get going."

"Really?" Nikki and Rachel spoke at the same time.

"I have business to take care of."

"Like what?" Nikki asked, and Rachel was content to let her do the badgering.

Getting to his feet, he gave his sister a patient but firm look. "I'll call you."

"When?"

"Later." He paused. "Might not see you till tomorrow though."

She folded her arms. "Fine."

"Knock off the attitude," he said, playfully tugging her hair again. "Or you'll carry your own bag upstairs."

"I'm doing it myself, anyway, so go."

Laughing, Barbara planted her palms on the table and pushed herself up. "I'm having a cup of coffee. If anyone else wants one, it's now or never."

"You mind walking me to the door first, Mrs. McAllister?" Matt asked quietly.

"Of course, but I think you might be old enough to call me Barbara now." She put an arm around his middle, appearing tiny next to him, and steered him toward the door separating the kitchen and dining room.

Rachel had already risen halfway out of her seat, then felt awkward because she'd wanted to walk Matt. "I'll get you situated, Nikki," she said, pretending that was her plan all along.

"Thanks." Nikki smiled. "I still wish y'all would let me pay for my room."

"Not going to happen." Her gaze automatically went to the back of Matt's head. He smiled at her over his shoulder before he pushed open the swinging door.

Hilda returned through the mudroom, followed by Jamie, whose gaze lit when she saw Nikki. "Hey." Then she noticed the dining room door still moving. Rachel was leading Nikki in the same direction. "Where's everyone going?" Jamie set the brown paper bag on the counter. "Did I miss everything?"

In spite of her crankiness at being bested by her mom, Rachel couldn't help but laugh. "Matt is leaving. Nikki is staying. I'm taking her to her room. We'll be right back. Hilda won't tell you anything before then."

Hilda smiled, shaking her head and already putting away groceries.

"Yeah, okay, I'll remember this, Rach. Next time all you get is a postcard from Europe," she called after them even though they'd left the kitchen.

"Europe?" Nikki said. "Is she kidding?"

"It's her job. She's a travel blogger."

"Wow. Cool."

"She lives here now…moved from L.A. last month," Rachel said absently, too busy sneaking a peek at her mom and Matt standing at the front door.

Neither of them spared her or Nikki a glance when they stopped for the small bag sitting at the foot of the stairs. Rachel grabbed it first. The duffel was light, maybe only three days' worth of clothes inside.

Her mother patted Matt's arm and she had that soft maternal smile full of concern and reassurance at the same time. A smile reserved for times when one of her children was having a rough go and she wanted to make it better but couldn't.

"I can take it."

"What?" Not paying attention, she nearly missed the first step but recovered quickly. "Oh, no problem."

"I don't know what they're talking about," Nikki whispered as they ascended the wide staircase together. "I really don't."

"That obvious, huh?" Rachel looked at her and sighed.

"What, you think I won't ask him what that's about?"

Rachel chuckled. "Will you tell me?"

"Depends. He is my brother. Half brother," she amended. "But he doesn't like it when I make the distinction."

"I noticed, and I'm not surprised." Rachel smiled, liking that Nikki was loyal and wouldn't rat him out. Because he'd return the favor in spades. If anything, he was loyal to a fault. "I'm so glad he has you. Matt is…he's just a great guy." Rachel blushed. "But you already know that."

"I do, but I still give him a hard time." Nikki sniffed. "I shouldn't. It's not his fault Wallace is a prick."

"Uh, yes, he is." Good word choice. "That man never deserved his wife or his son—that's for damn sure."

"Guess I'm the lucky one," Nikki said wryly, and Rachel wanted to kick herself yet again.

She was talking to his daughter, for God's sake. "I think you'll like your room," she said, quickening her pace. "It's small but it faces the Rockies, and it may snow tonight, which will be pretty."

Nikki's face lit. "I hope it does. I've never seen snow fall."

Rachel ushered her into the room, then went straight for the blinds. She opened them to show Nikki the view, but deep down she knew she wanted to catch a glimpse of Matt.

Her pulse leaped when she saw him heading for his truck. She hated that he wouldn't stay and refused to give a reason. Not that he owed her one. Maybe she was wrong to hope for more kisses in their future.

And then it hit her…the kiss might have meant nothing more than an apology for having left.

Another small piece of her heart chipped off as she watched him leave again.

9

MATT KNEW HE WAS TAKING a chance showing up at Rachel's front door and expecting her to go for a drive with him. She had a dude ranch to run, guests to worry about…and since it had snowed last night, their planned activities were probably shot to hell.

He had time to call her. He was still ten minutes away from the Sundance. Though at the speed he was driving, five might be more accurate. Breathing in deeply, he lifted his foot off the accelerator. The roads were relatively clear, no ice anyway, but that wasn't the point. He knew better than to drive fast on this road, hell, any road. It was plain stupid and reckless, and unfortunately matched his mood. He could lie to himself all he wanted that he wasn't that hotheaded guy anymore…until Wallace entered the mix.

Shit, he'd spent ten lousy minutes with the bastard this morning and he'd let Wallace get to him. The old man had made no bones about his indifference to Nikki. Said he hadn't acknowledged her before, why should he now. But he'd asked about Rosa, which pissed Matt off even more, and thank God Nikki hadn't been there to hear that.

The worst part of the morning was that nothing Wallace did or said had shocked Matt. So what kind of idiot did that make him? Why in the hell had he even considered that the asshole would change his stripes and do right by Nikki? Not one speck of logic existed for Matt to have made that leap. He had first-hand experience of Wallace's miserable failure as a father. As a husband. As a human being. For nearly nineteen years Matt had done everything he could to please his father…even now it made him sick to think of himself as a kid, practically kissing the man's boots trying to get his attention.

He realized he was speeding again, exhaled sharply, easing his foot off the pedal. Damn good thing he'd gotten rid of the Corvette last year. He'd only done it because of Nikki. She'd referred to the car as his coffin on wheels. Told him how cruel it was for him to come into her life and then be careless with his. Said it right to his face that if he did something foolish that ripped them apart, she'd hate him even in his grave.

She'd been good for him, made him give a damn again after his mother's death. And he was a total ass because every selfish inch of him wanted only to be alone with Rachel. Of course he'd ask Nikki to go with them. If she did, fine, but that's not what he wanted. Even after ten years, Rachel was like a soothing, addictive tonic. Being with her made everything better. His brain told him that was crazy thinking, but every other part of him clung to the certainty that accepting her friendship was the sanest thing he'd ever done.

The private road to the Sundance had been plowed. He took the turn easy, already feeling calmer knowing he was going to see her soon. She probably had another commitment. But he'd get to look into her pretty green eyes, bask in her smile, and if he was lucky, touch that silky soft skin of hers. His stupid heart started pounding like a junkie about to get a fix.

He parked his truck next to a small SUV and a red compact, rentals belonging to the guests, he figured. Then, instead of climbing out, he reached into his jacket pocket for his phone.

He hit speed dial for the cell number she'd given him. Then he put the phone to his ear and stared at the front of the house.

Rachel answered on the fourth ring, her voice a breathless whisper.

"Question," he said, relaxed, sinking back against the leather seat.

"Um, yes." Sounded like she was smiling.

"Your mama let you date, darlin'?"

"Depends."

"On?"

"What you have in mind."

"Well, my truck does have a big backseat...."

An upstairs curtain moved. "Matthew Gunderson, is that you lurking outside my house?"

"Depends." He tugged down the brim of his hat, thinking he might not mind a little phone sex as a warm-up. "You gonna call the sheriff?"

"Three's a crowd, silly cowboy." She laughed. "I'll be right down."

"Rachel, wait—"

She'd already hung up. Damn, why couldn't she be like most women...walk and talk at the same time?

He hit Nikki's number. He had to hurry and call her so she wouldn't think he was blowing her off. They'd spoken last night because she'd been excited to watch the snow come down. But he'd been distracted by what Lucy had told him about Wallace yesterday when she'd stopped by the Lone Wolf with groceries.

It had been good to see her, though Matt hated that she was really showing her age. Three years ago, with his mom so sick, the weeks he'd spent at the ranch had been a blur. Or maybe Lucy hadn't been so stooped and slow then. But she was still a spitfire, and they'd talked at the kitchen table for three hours while Wallace stayed locked in his office drinking.

Nikki didn't answer. Odd, because she was rarely separated

from her smartphone. He hoped that meant she was off having fun and left her a voice mail as he got out of the truck.

Rachel was already standing with the door open waiting for him by the time he made it across the gravel walkway. "Hurry up," she said, her arms wrapped around herself and shivering. "It's freezing."

"It's Montana and it's February, darlin'," he said, taking the porch steps two at a time, while reaching for his hat.

"Leave it on."

"What?"

"Your Stetson." She grabbed his arm when he stopped short, and drew him into the house.

"Because?"

She closed the door then turned around and leaned against it as if holding back the cold. "You know," she said, that teasing glint in her eyes. They seemed darker probably because of her snug black sweater, which molded every curve.

Turned out he didn't need phone sex to get warmed up. "Uh, nope, I don't."

She ducked to look behind him where the living room extended toward the den, then glanced toward the dining room and stairs. He hadn't seen anyone but he heard voices.

"Are you here for Nikki?" she asked, which was weird because why would that be a secret?

"No," he said, "for you. What's the deal with the Stetson?"

She grabbed the lapels of his suede jacket and pulled him down while she pushed up onto her toes. "You're too damn handsome for your own good," she murmured close to his mouth, her warm sweet breath mingling with his startled exhale.

"You gonna tease me or kiss me?" His voice came out a gruff rasp. Her house, her rules, but only for a few more seconds.

"Kiss you." She smiled. "Just not here." She let him go.

He stumbled back a step and palmed the crown to keep from losing the hat. "To be clear...the Stetson turns you on, and without it, you'd kick me to the curb."

"Something like that," she said with a cheeky grin and moved toward the approaching voices.

"Funny," he said, keeping his voice low. "I was thinking how I'd like to see you without that sweater."

She jerked a look at him, her lips parted and her eyes blazing with desire.

He touched her hand. "Come for a drive with me."

"Give me a few minutes."

"Whatever time you need." He smiled. "But take too long and I might start begging."

"Tempting," she muttered, then at the sound of the swinging door to the kitchen, pasted on a smile for the trail of chatty women streaming through the dining room toward the foyer.

Hell, seeing them reminded him. How, in the span of a second, could he have forgotten about Nikki? He'd have to include her in the outing. Rachel would understand. Or better he level with his sister. The risk there was that she could feel neglected and want to return to Houston.

"Hi, Matt." It was a chorus. Several of the women obviously knew his name.

He recalled the tall blonde, Sandy, only because she'd gotten him a beer the other night. He whipped off his hat. "Mornin', everyone."

They were all smiles and fake tans, and they were probably very nice women but he still had to fight the impulse to run and hide in the barn.

Before any of them could strike up a conversation with him, Rachel called for their attention and started reviewing the day's activities. Nikki and Jamie emerged from the back. He hoped they'd been hanging out in Cole's office or else it was a good bet they'd heard him and Rachel.

Nah, it was all good because Nikki looked surprised to see him. He was just being paranoid.

"I didn't know you were coming," Nikki said, and motioned for him to meet her in the living room away from the others.

"I left you a voice mail."

"We don't have plans, do we?" she asked, glancing back, he assumed to Jamie, who'd waved then disappeared.

"No. I figured I'd check if you and Rachel were interested in taking a drive with me."

"Is she going?"

"Said she would."

"Good. I'm not." She elbowed him. "I *know* you don't mind."

He shook his head, recognizing the mischievous gleam in her eye. She was hoping he and Rachel would end up doing a little boot-knocking. Hell, so was he, but he wasn't about to admit it.

Nikki grinned. "I have a playdate with Jamie and two of the guests."

"Doing what?"

"She's showing us how to cross-country ski."

"You don't have the right clothes. You'll freeze your backside off."

"Don't worry, Dad," she said with an eye roll. "I have it covered."

"You going shopping?" He reached for his wallet in his back pocket.

"Stop it, Matt."

"What?"

Her hands on her hips, she glared at him. "You try to give me so much as a dollar, I will be so pissed at you."

"Don't get your feathers ruffled. You can't wear jeans. You'll get 'em caked with snow. When it melts the wet denim will stick to your skin, then freeze again. And ski gear isn't cheap."

Some of her bravado slipped and she moistened her lips.

"I'm not going to buy a bunch of clothes I can't wear when I get home. If my jeans freeze, I'll change."

They stared at each other without speaking. Matt was aware that the others could hear them if they were so inclined. He didn't need to say anything, since Nikki knew he was hoping she'd like Blackfoot Falls and consider eventually making the Lone Wolf her home. He also knew that her finances were tight. Being here meant she wasn't making tips at the bar where she worked.

He dropped his gaze to his wallet. "How about I give you a few hundred, just in case?" he asked, quietly.

She sighed. "You want kids, go make babies."

"You're more ornery than a bull."

"And yet you continue to forget." She spun around and walked away.

He watched her race up the stairs without a look back. He'd hurt her pride. Again. It wasn't as if he didn't admire her independence and her hard work to preserve it. But he wanted so much to help make her life easier. The money—he had so much, and it meant nothing to him. Nikki knew that.

"Don't worry," Rachel said, coming to stand beside him as he watched Nikki disappear down the upstairs hall. "Between Jamie and I, she'll have the proper clothes to wear. I've already laid a few things out for her to choose from."

He glanced toward the foyer, saw that the guests had dispersed, then looked down at the top of her head and smiled at the purple streak.

She looped an arm through his. "You ready? Before Trace ambushes me and begs out of taking some of our guests on a trail ride."

"Let's get outta here."

Barbara McAllister appeared at the top of the stairs, and they stopped in the foyer. She looked pretty in gray wool slacks and a cream sweater. Auburn hair similar to Rachel's skimmed her shoulders.

"Wow, Mom, where are you going?"

She seemed startled. "I thought you'd left with the others."

"They didn't need me so I'm playing hooky with Matt for a while."

"You look nice," he said to Barbara.

"Thank you." She blushed, just like her daughter.

"So where are you going?" Rachel asked again.

"To meet a friend, then run errands." She hurried down the stairs, keeping her gaze on her feet. "I left a couple pairs of insulated ski pants on my bed for Nikki if she's interested. They aren't trendy but she is closer to my height than yours." She reached the foyer and glanced at her watch. "I'm sorry. I really have to scoot."

"Where's your coat?" A slight frown puckered Rachel's brows.

"Oh, right. I'll go through the mudroom." Barbara flashed a smile. "See you later."

Rachel stared after her for a long minute. "That's the fourth time I've seen her with makeup since Thanksgiving. And did you notice she never answered where she was going?"

Laughing, Matt slipped an arm around her shoulders. "You're as bad with your mom as I am with Nikki."

She squinted up at him. "You hush."

He caught her chin, tilting it up, and pressed his lips to hers. They immediately relaxed, turned soft and yielding, and he considered that now might be a good time to sneak into her room. Then he remembered that Nikki and Jamie were in the house. Hilda was probably in the kitchen.

But when Rachel's mouth opened, his mind went blank. The tip of her tongue slipped out to touch his lower lip and his entire body tightened with need. He caught her hips, bracketing the tempting curves with his hands, and pulled her into him.

She let out a sexy whimper that spoke directly to his cock. He sucked the throaty sound into his mouth, and shuddered when she melted against him. Her arms wound around his neck, and he'd moved his hands to her firm round backside before it struck him that he was pushing his luck. One of her brothers could walk in on them. He doubted they wanted to see Matt shoving up their sister's sweater, looking for a taste of those sweet full breasts pressing against his chest.

With a great deal of effort, he loosened her arms from his neck and set her away from him. "We have to go."

"Where?" She blinked away the dazed expression, then bent to swoop his hat off the floor.

Hell, he hadn't noticed it had fallen. "I don't know." He raked a hand through his hair, then resettled the Stetson. "Out of here. Jacket?"

"Jacket," she repeated, but plainly without understanding. She drew in a shaky breath, then her eyes lit with awareness. "Right. That way," she said, hitching her thumb toward the kitchen, which led to the coat hooks in the mudroom.

"I'll meet you at the truck."

She just nodded and took off.

He walked with purpose, head down, straight to the truck. Moments later she joined him. She opened the passenger door and hopped in, her face flushed, her hair a mass of sexy curls, her eyes sparkling like it was Christmas.

"What took you so long?" Matt inserted the key sitting uselessly in his hand and ignited the engine.

"I was less than a minute. Jeez, I didn't even brush my hair or grab my purse," she said, grinning. "Or put on my jacket." She tried to now, arching her spine as she pushed her arm into one of the sleeves.

His gaze moved over the thrust of her breasts, and without thinking he touched one through her sweater.

She froze, but didn't push him away. She looked over at him, the desire in her eyes matching his own. He indulged himself a moment longer, felt her nipple harden through her bra and the soft wool. How long had he wanted to see her naked, feel her body hot and needy moving beneath his.

No, he hadn't thought about her steadily over the past decade, but the years didn't seem to matter once he'd laid eyes on her again. Right now it felt as if Rachel had always been the woman he truly wanted. The ache in his belly and the longing in his heart made all the others seem like substitutes. He hadn't used them. They were all more than willing. Some of them too willing to slip between the sheets of a bull-riding champion. That aside, he hadn't once understood his yearning to find a surrogate for the woman he'd never be able to have.

"Oh, boy, we really should go." Rachel's chest heaved unsteadily beneath his hand. "Like five minutes ago."

The truck was idling. Good thing the engine was quiet, although who knew what kind of attention they'd drawn. He lowered his hand and glanced around. No one in sight. Cold temperatures kept most of the men inside the barns and stables, or readying the calving sheds. And his windows were heavily tinted, but no need to feed speculation.

He reversed the truck, and noticed Rachel scanning the front of the house, probably hoping no one saw them.

"I'm sorry," he said. "I shouldn't have touched you like that. Not here."

Laughing, she finished shrugging into her jacket. "Thank you for the qualification."

"Full disclosure, darlin'." He turned his eyes to the driveway and away from temptation, before he made a complete ass out of himself. "I'm touching you again. You can count on it."

_10_

RACHEL ADJUSTED THE VENTS, aiming the heated air away from her face, away from her, period. Her cheeks were flushed since she couldn't stop thinking about him touching her, and her body was still throbbing where he already had. She shivered anyway.

"Cold?" He reached for the controls.

"No." She swatted his hand. "I'm roasting, thanks to you."

He smiled slyly. "Should've left the jacket off."

She groaned when she saw that she was hugging the quilted down fabric to her chest as if it would protect her from him. "And I forgot my gloves. I assume we're getting out at some point."

"Take mine." He indicated a pair sitting on the console. Definitely not work gloves. These were made of fine brown leather, and not something one found in Blackfoot Falls.

"They're too big. Anyway, you should be wearing them."

He just shrugged. "We can go back for yours."

"No way. I was lucky to escape the first time. So, where are we going?"

"Up to Weaver Ridge. I want to have a look at the cabin and piece of land my mom left me."

"Oh." She vaguely knew the area. His mother was a Weaver and the land had been in her family forever, just like the McAllisters' and Gundersons' land. "Too much snow, don't you think?"

"Only four inches last night." He waved at the driver of the oncoming truck. "I think that was Roy Tisdale. He still a deputy?"

"Yes, he's been investigating the thefts around the area." She sighed. "Our missing horse trailer among other items."

He shot her a glance before negotiating the curve that would take them west to Weaver Ridge. "Your trailer was stolen?"

"The big one. An Exiss."

"Damn. When?"

"Last August. Since then other ranches have reported missing equipment and saddles. And the strange part is that it all started with Mrs. Clements misplacing a four-wheeler. She called Noah—" Rachel turned to look at him, her breath catching at his rugged profile, the way his light brown hair curled at his collar. He used to wear it so short she'd thought his hair was straight. "Did you know that Noah Calder is our sheriff?"

"Yeah, I heard he came back. He worked as a cop in Chicago, right?"

She nodded. "I don't know how he did it. First the army, then college, a job in Chicago…he was gone a long time. Coming back had to be quite an adjustment. Blackfoot Falls is still…"

"Blackfoot Falls," he finished when her voice trailed off, his attention firmly on the road ahead. They were approaching the foothills. He needed to focus on driving, yet she sensed his mood had shifted. Did he think she was dissing Blackfoot Falls? "Tell me more about the thefts," he said. "Was anything recovered?"

"Yes and no. Some things showed up a few days later in a field or near the property where the item was taken. Initially Noah thought someone might be messing with him."

"How could anyone take a trailer that size from the Sundance without being seen."

"It was the first theft, and it happened at night. We'd officially opened for guests a couple weeks earlier, so we were busy and not paying attention." She really did like him with the black Stetson. He looked so damn sexy with the brim pulled low that she shivered. "Avery Phelps, along with a few others, were not happy with us bringing in tourists and tried to blame the Sundance for the thefts."

"Figures. I bet Wallace was one of the bellyachers."

She didn't respond, unwilling to enter a discussion about her brothers' suspicion Matt's father was somehow involved. "I think Noah came back because his sisters left and his parents were here alone, but now that he has a girlfriend in New York, I don't know how that will play out. He was gone a lot through the holidays."

"New York?" Matt's brows went up. If he'd noticed she'd purposely changed the subject, he didn't let on. "How did that happen?"

"The evil McAllisters and their dude ranch happened."

"Ah." He smiled. "Another guest? First Cole, then Jesse and then Noah. You're an evil woman."

"Wrong order. Noah bit the dust before Jesse. Technically Alana never really made it to guest status. He headed her off in town. And excuse me, but I take no responsibility, so don't 'evil woman' me." She shifted, angling more toward him, then laid her cheek against the seat back so she could stare at him. "Although I do take credit for getting my brothers off their butts and into serious relationships."

He lifted a brow at her in amusement.

"What? Somebody better get moving and give my mom a few grandbabies."

"So you elected Cole and Jesse."

"Trace, married? Come on."

"And you?"

The idea startled a laugh out of her. "I was holding out to

be Mrs. Gunderson." It was a joke, of course, though not one she would've made had she stopped to think.

Matt narrowed his focus on the road. He actually seemed afraid to look at her.

"I was kidding, Matt. Jeez, you know how girls are when they're sixteen." She decided she was better off not staring at him, and swung her knees front and center.

"Can't say that I do."

"Quit being ornery."

"Hell, I've never figured out a female yet."

She bit her lip. "You know I had a crush on you and like a typical teenage girl, I daydreamed about getting married and having kids and all that nonsense." She waited for a reaction, which he stubbornly refused to give. "Don't worry," she said, sighing. "That was ten years ago. Now all I want is your body."

He actually blushed. "Dammit, Rachel." Chuckling, he rubbed the back of his neck, something he'd always done when he was caught off guard. "You're still a handful."

"Um…" She was about to say something else she really shouldn't.

"Yes?" He slid a look over her mouth, then lower to her breasts.

He sure had recovered quickly, and now she was the one squeezing her thighs together, praying her cheeks were just warm and not pink. God, she hoped the cabin was accessible. It would be dusty and stuffy but as long as it had a roof and walls to give them privacy, they could air out the sucker, light a fire, and she'd be happy.

They veered left then started to climb. It had been ages since she'd been anywhere near Weaver Ridge but she knew they were close. Unfortunately, there was considerably more snow up here than around the Sundance. Not horrible for February, but still. "What do you think, ten minutes away?"

"If memory serves." He nodded slowly, clearly not thinking about their ETA. "Might as well get it over with." The same edginess in his voice she'd noticed earlier made her sit straighter. "I had a long talk with Lucy yesterday. Wallace is dying."

"Matt, I'm sorry."

He snorted. "You think I give a shit?"

"Yes, he's still your father, and you're not like him. You're human." She drew in a harsh breath. Second time today she'd spoken without thinking. "That last part...completely uncalled for. I apologize."

Reaching over, he laid a hand on her thigh. "Hey, you know better than anyone how much I hated the bastard. All the crappy stuff he did and said, I eventually let roll off my back. But the way he treated my mother..."

She pressed her palm to the back of his much-larger hand. His tan couldn't hide the small scars that came from working a ranch and riding bulls. "Do you still hate him?"

He hesitated, returning his hand to the steering wheel. "No. I don't feel anything."

Though unconvinced that was true, Rachel kept her opinion to herself. "Have you told Nikki?"

"Not yet."

"How do you think she'll take it?"

"Can't say. We knew he was either sick or headed for a drunk tank before the trip." He steered them onto a gravel road covered with snow, and shifted gears. "Even then, she ran hot and cold about coming."

"How did you find her?"

"My mom."

Rachel gasped. "She knew? For how long?"

"Twenty years, maybe."

"Oh, God."

"Yep. Never said a word to Wallace."

"But she told you."

"Only because she was dying. Took me another year to get over it and look up Nikki." He glanced at her, his mouth drawn tight. "Not proud of the year-long sulk, by the way."

"Jeez, your mother had just passed away. Cut yourself a break."

He smiled a little. "I made her a promise to prove Nikki is a Gunderson and included in Wallace's estate. But keep that between us. Nikki doesn't know and she'd be pissed. She doesn't want anything from him other than closure. I'd like to see her eventually take over the Lone Wolf."

Rachel sure hadn't seen that coming. Nor did she see Nikki living here. "Does that mean you're through with ranching?"

"Nope. I've got money set aside for a spread. I can't rodeo forever. As a matter of fact, I don't see myself doing it too much longer."

"But you're popular and winning titles like crazy. Frankly, I don't understand why you're not up to your neck in endorsement contracts."

"Don't want 'em."

Rachel let out a short laugh that ended in a sigh. She was a little jealous of his earning power. Not for herself, but for the Sundance. Her family would be worry-free with the kind of money he could make in two months. "You can't find one product you agree with?"

"Guess I'm not the mugging-for-the-camera type. That's what the companies all want. If I had kids to put through college maybe I'd give in and invest the money for them." He shrugged a shoulder. "I haven't been too stupid about saving. I might be a hot ticket now, but the fame will dry up the day I leave that chute for the last time. So will the money."

She didn't agree. He could hang on to endorsements for quite a while. Rodeo fans were loyal, and from what she'd seen online, everybody in that world loved him. On top of that, he was good-looking. What she really wondered was why he seemed willing to give up the lifestyle.

A horrible thought occurred to her. "Did you lie yesterday when I asked if you were all right? Are you hurt?"

"What?" He frowned at her, then turned back to the gravel road. The snow was deeper out here, still dripping from spruce branches and climbing a foot up the aspens. "No."

"Maybe we should turn around," she said, hearing the grind of snow in the wheel wells while the truck struggled for traction.

"We're okay. It's not far. Why did you ask if I was hurt? Is that what the media is saying?"

"No, but most guys in your position would be dreading the day they had to leave the circuit. When they do, isn't it mainly because of age or injury?"

"Usually. I want to raise rodeo stock. Might as well get a ranch going while I'm young and healthy enough to enjoy it."

She smiled. Matt was still the same in many ways. Sensible, sensitive, even-tempered, an all-around good guy. He hadn't let fame or money go to his head. Or let his troubled relationship with his father make him bitter. She was really curious about why he wouldn't take over the Lone Wolf, since he wanted to raise livestock. But she wouldn't ask now. Driving was tricky and she needed to let him concentrate.

The one thing that had gotten her a bit down was his wanting Nikki to run the operation. Although Rachel couldn't see it, she had nothing against his sister taking over. It was more personal. Rachel had to face the fact that Matt had only wanted to stick around to give Nikki a chance to assimilate. It had nothing to do with Rachel.

"You worried about my driving?" he asked. "I can still handle snow."

She shook her head. "I was just thinking…"

"Oh, man. You used to get me in trouble by 'just thinking.'"

"Hey…who kidnapped who this morning?" Catching a glimpse of the cabin, she straightened. The area didn't look too bad. Yes, lots of snow, but much of it had blown past the clearing. "When was the last time you were here?"

"After Mom's funeral. I have two generations of great-grandparents buried in the back…. I came by to tell them I was sorry she was put in the same cemetery as the Gunder-sons and not with them." His mouth twisted in a self-conscious smile. "Funny how you do weird crap after someone close to you dies."

"I know." She laid a hand on his thigh, and he picked it up and kissed her palm.

"Yeah, you do."

The truck bumped over a rock that had him pulling his hand back to control the wheel. They both knew what it felt like to lose a beloved parent. Matt had been there for her when she was fourteen and her father died of cancer. Now that she thought about it, their relationship had begun the day Matt had found her angry and crying in Elk Valley a week after her dad's funeral.

She'd swiped Cole's rifle, believing that target practice would help ease her pent-up grief and rage at the unfairness of life. Without knowing where she was headed, she'd ridden her horse as if the devil himself were after her. She'd gotten off a shot at a tree branch when Matt appeared out of the woods. He was a senior, and she and her friends thought he was cute, but she hadn't known him, not really. No one did. He'd always stuck to himself and gone straight home after school.

Remembering that day made her shudder. If she'd been aim-ing lower…if he hadn't let her know he was there…

He stopped the truck, turned off the engine. "What's wrong?"

"Oh, crap." She frowned at the front of the cabin. "Look at all the snow blocking the door."

"Must've been windy up here last night."

Shade from the towering pines didn't help. The snow hadn't had a chance to melt and had accumulated. "We won't be able to get inside."

"Maybe there's a broken window." He lifted the brim of his hat, squinting at the two-story log cabin. "When I was a kid I thought the place was gigantic, but it can't be more than two thousand square feet. Seems to be holding up well. You too cold to get out?"

"Pfft." She waved a hand. "I'm a hearty Montana woman. You think a little snow is going to stop me?"

Grinning, he lifted the door handle. "I'll remind you of that later."

She beat him out of the truck but couldn't compete in racing him to the cabin. She hadn't exercised in a while and it showed. The snow was deeper than she'd imagined, swallowing her footfalls, making each step so heavy and awkward that she felt like a total klutz.

Trailing the path he left behind by a humbling distance, she fought her way to the cabin, simply happy to keep the huffing and puffing down to a minimum.

"Are you all right?"

Smiling sweetly, she said, "Peachy."

He retraced his steps, meeting her partway, then scooped her into his arms.

Laughing, rather than taste the bitterness of her dissolving pride, she said. "This is just mean."

"I'm being mean?"

She looped her arms around his neck, careful not to knock off his hat as he carried her to the cabin where he'd cleared away the snow. "I could've made it on my own."

"Sweetheart, you will always make it on your own," he said, a strange tone to his voice.

"You say that like it's a bad thing." She wasn't joking. He'd almost sounded disappointed.

"No, it's not. You've always been strong and independent, and I'm glad you haven't changed." He smiled, but he seemed just a little sad. Maybe it wasn't about her or them, but his father. "Grab my hat."

She caught the back brim just as he lowered his head and gave her an open-mouth kiss that stole what scant breath she had left. His tongue slowly swept inside, touched hers, then continued its exploration. He was in no hurry, more intent on doing a thorough job than moving on. She clung to him, soaking up his seductive heat, smelling the faint scent of soap and clean male flesh and feeling herself slowly melt into him.

Finally, she dragged her mouth away because she really was out of breath. "You can put me down now."

"I want to keep you right here." He held her tighter to his chest. "For a week, a month." He kissed her hair and quietly murmured, "Forever."

This wasn't real. Not his words or the way he cradled her as if he truly didn't want to let go. It was the grief talking. He needed someone safe to hold on to, someone who would hold him. He could deny it all he wanted, but he was affected by the confirmation his father was terminal. Maybe a less-sensitive man could ignore the blow, but not Matt.

"Let's find a way inside," she said, massaging his scalp below the hat.

He drew back, his closed eyes opening in degrees and reflecting the blue of the sky. His heart beat fast and hard against the side of her breast. "We'll get in."

She traced a fingertip over his bottom lip. "Or maybe that's asking for trouble."

His smile was slow and so damn sexy that her insides quivered. "I'm counting on it," he said, and carefully let her slide down his body.

Even through the barrier of their layered clothing, she felt his arousal pressed against her belly, felt tiny jolts of electricity along her spine. "I hate this."

"What?" he asked, concern in his eyes as he gently arranged her hair away from her face.

"Me living at the Sundance, you staying at the Lone Wolf. The whole no-privacy issue stinks."

"Ah. Been thinking about that myself." He kissed the side of her neck. "Kalispell isn't far."

"We can't. Not today. I'm helping decorate for the dance." She sighed at the featherlike feel of his lips heating her skin.

"No, not today. I have to talk to Nikki about Wallace. What about tonight after you're done? Or tomorrow after the dance?"

"Definite possibilities."

He briefly kissed her. "Wait here."

"Where are you going?" Hugging herself, trying to ward off the cold void he'd left, she watched him head in the direction of the truck. Was he getting condoms?

Then she saw that he was only trying to avoid a large snowdrift and circle around to the back of the cabin. The wind had been blowing from the west so the rear was much clearer and more accessible. He was probably searching for that broken window.

She glanced around at the barren trees and pines in varying shades of green. Not the ideal spot for a ranch—too hilly—but the place would be beautiful with wildflowers and new leaves by mid-May. Such a shame the cabin was sitting vacant.

After what seemed like forever, Matt approached her from the other side so she knew he'd made it all the way around. Snow sat on his Stetson and shoulders, and he looked like a man who'd lost a small battle. Maybe it was just as well they couldn't get inside. They'd already waited this long and she didn't want their first time to be about him hiding from grief.

"Oh, well, we tried." She dusted the snow off his shoulders. "There's still Kalispell...."

He winked at her as he took her hand, leading her down the path he'd just made.

11

MATT PRESENTED THE OPEN window with a bow. "Did you really think I couldn't get us inside? What little faith you have in me." Nothing could be further from the truth. Rachel had been his rock, the persistent voice in his head telling him he could do anything he wanted, no matter how many times Wallace chipped away at his confidence.

She lifted up to brush her lips across his mouth. "You're my hero."

It was the other way around. But if he pointed it out, she'd only argue. He started to pull her in for a more satisfying kiss, but didn't trust himself to stop. Knowing they were going to have some privacy was already getting him worked up. He gave her a quick hug, then searched the wood trim for splinters.

The cabin was well built with thick walls and insulated panes of glass. Matt was glad he hadn't had to break in, but he suspected he might've warped the track while trying to loosen the jammed window. Easy enough to repair, and if not, he didn't really give a crap. Especially when he turned back to Rachel shading her sparkling green eyes from the sun, her hair a brilliant auburn blaze tumbling over her shoulders. She looked beautiful. But she always did.

Stomping his foot, he made sure the snow was packed hard

under his feet before he gave her a boost up to the window. He glanced down at his boots. His good Moraes boots. They weren't trashed yet because the snow was dry and he kept shaking it off. But he'd had no business wearing them to come up here. This is what he got for being impulsive and tearing out of the house. No, for letting Wallace push his buttons.

"You ready?" he asked, interlocking his fingers.

"I think I can climb up on my own."

"I'm sure you can. But would you let me help you?" This was so Rachel. Never giving up, never asking for help, no matter how high the odds against her. Since she was a kid she'd been a ball of energy, always moving forward, trying with her last breath to reach her goal.

"Yes," she said, her smile unexpectedly shy. "Thank you."

He lowered his hands, and she stepped one foot into them. She heaved herself up to the window and briefly perched on the ledge, drawing her knees up to her chest. Carefully she swung around and let herself inside.

"There's furniture in here," she said, sticking her head out the window. "I'm not sure what…everything is covered with sheets. Here." She offered her hand.

"It's better if you just stand clear."

She moved back, and he hoisted himself up.

The interior of the cabin was warmer than he expected so he figured it was worth trying to close the window again. It stuck twice and wouldn't go down all the way, but close enough.

"Did you know this stuff was here?" Rachel walked through the living room, peeking under the sheets.

"I vaguely recall my mom saying that some of the rooms were left intact." He glanced around, saw that even an old piano remained in the corner, and a coat tree stood near the front door.

"This couch is in good shape. So are the chairs."

He was more interested in the couch and started to yank off the sheet.

"Wait." Rachel's warning was too late.

Dust particles fluttered through the air making them both cough. He cussed between coughing bouts, while she laughed.

"Really smooth," she said, flapping a hand to clear the dust.

He caught her wrist, ignored her squeal of protest and pulled her toward him. When she realized he meant to kiss her, she quit fighting him and slid her arms around his neck. Her freezing hands were pressed to the skin under his jacket collar, but he didn't care. He'd warm her up soon enough.

He kissed the corner of her mouth, felt her lips tremble. "You still cold? I'm not sure about using the fireplace but we can try."

"No, let's not risk it." She tilted her head back to look at his face, while pressing her body into him. They really had to get rid of the bulky jackets. "Think we should look upstairs?"

"I believe the bedrooms are empty. I'll go check." He kissed her hard and quick, then resisted the urge to run up the stairs. No telling if they needed work.

But they felt solid under his boots and he used the time to get out of his jacket. After confirming all four bedrooms were without furniture, he returned to the living room. Rachel had rolled up the sheet from the couch and tucked it under the piano bench. She looked up and smiled.

"No luck upstairs." Remembering his hat, he tossed it along with the jacket onto a chair near the fireplace.

"Oh, well, at least this is in good shape." She pressed down on the brown-plaid seat cushion.

"Sure is ugly."

"But no dust."

"You need help with your jacket?" he asked, walking toward her.

She didn't say anything, just watched him approach as she unzipped and pulled her arms free of the sleeves.

He was already getting hard, and he hadn't even touched her yet. Or seen what was under that black sweater. Didn't matter really. He was alone with Rachel, and that's what he'd wanted most. Part of him still couldn't believe she was here in Blackfoot Falls. He'd imagined she would be anywhere but at the Sundance.

Her tongue slipped out to moisten her lips. He took the jacket from her and threw it at the chair. This was a moment he'd dreamed about—his desire for her had been years in the making.

Matt wrapped her in his arms and held her against his chest. She smelled so damn good. He'd always noticed a hint of vanilla around her, even when he'd been too horny and fueled by teenage hormones to care about the little things. Breathing her in, he hugged her tighter, then leaned back just enough to look at her face.

Her cheeks were flushed, her eyes bright, her lips slightly parted. The sun shining through the window lit up her hair and was starting to warm her skin. Though he figured he might have something to do with that, too. She sure had that effect on him.

"What?" she said, her lips twitching. "Why are you smiling like that?"

"We're finally alone. I have you in my arms. Why wouldn't I be smiling?" He kissed her, sliding his hands down her back until he found the hem of her sweater.

Slowly, he lifted it, giving her a moment to process what he was about to do. She gave a small jerk, breaking the kiss.

"You okay?"

"Better than okay," she said as her eyes drifted closed.

He skimmed his palm over her silky skin, let the tips of his fingers trail her delicate spine. He unfastened her bra, and cupped her bare breast. Her eyes opened and her warm breath whooshed out with a soft startled gasp that touched something inside of him. She'd known they were headed for this moment. The little minx had even baited him. But for all her new sophistication, in some ways, she was still that teenage girl testing boundaries in a sweet tangle of impatient determination and naïveté.

She'd hate the observation, deny it, tell him he was insane, he thought as he thumbed her taut nipple. The reality of what he was doing floored him. This was a first…he'd never touched her naked breasts before. Years ago, when they'd horsed around in Mill Creek, she'd worn a swimsuit. He'd wanted to slide his fingers beneath the fabric—God, how desperately he'd wanted to touch her—but he hadn't dared.

He settled his lips on hers, then adjusted his head so he could seek all of her mouth. She accepted his exploration with a whispery sigh that made his heart pump faster and his cock leap.

Heat roared through him. His body tightened with need, and it took everything he had not to lay her on the couch, spread her legs and bury himself inside of her. He'd sworn he'd take things slow, make their first time together memorable, give their lovemaking the tenderness it deserved….

Moving his hand away from her breast, he gentled the kiss. But she wasn't having that. She strained upward to keep their mouths joined. He had to act, or he wouldn't be able to trust himself. He lifted his head out of her reach, and she stared up at him as if he'd just cut off her air supply.

"That last night," Rachel said softly, and he met her eyes. "Remember I was going to sneak out and we were supposed to meet at the grove of aspens behind the calving shed…?"

He did all he could not to wince. Yeah, he remembered. It had been the painful night he'd left Blackfoot Falls.

"Earlier in the day I'd made up my mind that I was going to lose my virginity to you that night."

"Ah, Rachel—"

"Shh, no." She put a finger to his lips. "Don't say anything. I just wanted you to know."

With a heaviness in his chest, he wondered how long she'd

waited for him out there in the cold. Wondered if he hadn't climbed into his old truck, would he have tried to find comfort in her body? After that final explosive fight with Wallace, Matt might've gone against his own principles, taken what she offered. And he would've hated himself.

"I'm sorry," he whispered.

"I told you to be quiet." She pressed her body against his, pulling him into a kiss and urging the hand he held under her sweater back up to her breast.

Her beaded nipple teased his palm. He gently kneaded, learned the texture and feel of her, the pearled nub, the silky skin surrounding it. But that wasn't enough—he wanted to look at her. Taste her.

She unbuttoned his shirt and slipped her trembling hand inside, skimming his belly, grazing his nipple…touching the scars.

Matt drew back. The movement was subtle, but it wasn't a reflex. He'd never done that with a woman before. Not that he was aware of, and the scarred flesh hadn't made him particularly self-consciousness. Most of the wounds had healed well, and hell, they came with the territory.

He kept kissing her, hoping she hadn't noticed his withdrawal. But she had. He could feel it in the subdued pressure of her lips, the tentativeness of her touch. Yet what did he expect? This was Rachel. Even after ten years, she still knew him. Better than most anyone else, he suspected.

"The scars don't bother me," she said. "If that worries you. I just hate that you were hurt."

Staring into the heartfelt concern in her eyes brought him instant clarity. His reaction had everything to do with Rachel. He didn't care about being marked, but he was ashamed of what some of the scars represented. Proof that Wallace's blood flowed through his veins. Proof Matt had that same hot temper and mean streak if he didn't keep himself in check. He'd been reckless those first years on his own, getting into bar fights, starting them when he was in a foul mood.

"Matt?" She cupped his face in her soft hands. "You want to talk?"

He slowly shook his head, pulled her wrists to her sides and lifted her sweater. She was so damn perfect he couldn't breathe, couldn't stop staring.

"Yes, I still have freckles," she said with a nervous laugh.

"You're beautiful," he murmured, and lowered his head.

AT THE BAREST TOUCH of his tongue on her nipple, Rachel nearly slid to the floor. If she didn't get a grip, he would think she was still a virgin. He rolled his tongue over her other breast then brought his head up and claimed her mouth with a fierceness that pushed her over the edge of reason.

She fisted his hair but let him do whatever he wanted. And God, he wanted all of her. He couldn't seem to settle in any one spot for long. His lips moved to her chin and jaw, and then the tender spot below her ear. Only when her sweater slipped down, did he lift his head.

"This has to go," he said, his voice a rough rasp, his eyes like she'd never seen them before.

She'd always loved the mesmerizing light blue, but this midnight color really worked, too. In answer, she pulled up the hem and then let him lift the sweater off the rest of the way.

"You, too," she ordered, and gestured when he reached for her.

Immediately he jerked the flannel shirt off his shoulders, but she knew the exact moment he remembered the scars. He wavered a second, blinked, then finished the task. His face, though, was completely unreadable, so unlike his younger version, and that made her ache.

She got rid of her bra, boots and jeans in a mad rush, leaving her in tiny blue panties, while he stripped down to black boxer briefs. She wanted to just stare at him, take in all the amazing changes that had transformed his body. But more than anything she longed to feel him. Now. He must have felt the same because before she could even blink he'd lifted her bride-style and put her on the couch. Without missing a beat, she pulled him down on top of her so he settled between the V of her legs.

He kissed her leisurely and thoroughly, their tongues swirling and mating, their pounding hearts ignoring the unhurried pace he'd tried to set. When he drew his palm down her naked back, she shivered, felt goose bumps surface.

"Cold?" he murmured against her mouth.

"Turned on."

The next thing she knew he'd scooted down. After a quick kiss to her inner thigh, he tugged down her panties and pulled them off. He stood to get out of his boxers, and her breath caught. Sunlight shimmered off the smooth tanned skin of his chest and shoulders.

Her gaze followed as he peeled down his briefs, his erection so hard the head brushed his stomach. She swallowed, as she looked at him, amazed that all the times she'd imagined him naked, her imagination hadn't been nearly enough.

With a groan that made her insides tight, he grabbed his jeans and searched out his wallet. Once he had the red packet in hand, he tossed the rest away and settled back down on the couch, kneeling between her thighs. "I'm almost afraid to touch you," he said. "You've been a part of my dreams for so long, I don't want to suddenly wake up."

She arched up, resting on her elbows. "Come on down here and I'll show you just how real I am."

His smile made her melt, and the heat of his body on hers made her shiver. She found his mouth and they met and parted and met again, each time a new discovery.

She couldn't stop her gasp when his hand slid up the inside of her thigh. She rose to meet him, and he thrust his tongue inside her mouth, two fingers slipping into the moist heat of her sex.

"Rachel, I can't wait." he whispered as he moved back to look at her.

"Me, too."

He groaned, and she might have whimpered when his fingers moved away, but then she heard the tearing of the packet, and she watched, panting, as he sheathed himself.

When he looked at her again, his dark eyes were unblinking. He shifted up, looming above her, his muscled arms on either side of her chest. He took her in a ferocious kiss, a claiming, and then he rebalanced, freeing one hand.

He entered her slowly. She could feel it was difficult for him, that he was using everything he had to keep himself in check. But she was in no mood to be careful.

She threw her leg over his back and pulled him down, until he slid into her body and filled her completely.

His gasp was mixed with laughter, but only for a moment. When their eyes met again, it was like a flash fire. She had to struggle to keep hers open because she wanted to see everything. The tendons stretching in his neck, the beads of sweat on his forehead. The way he looked at her as if she were the only woman he'd ever wanted.

Rachel cried out when he shifted forward. The angle was perfect with her heel digging into the small of his back. She tried to keep him right there, but he pulled out—not all the way, but enough to make her moan in protest. He touched her hair then thrust into her again. She tensed, close to breaking point, as he moved deep and slow inside her, convinced she wouldn't be able to take this much longer. Each time he thrust forward, his erection rubbed her clit and sent a jolt running through her. It had never felt like this before, like being ridden by lightning.

"God, Rachel, I can't last much—"

His mouth covered hers, kissing her with a savage hunger

that stole her breath. His body went rigid, then arched against her. He murmured her name again, and she held on to his arms so tightly he'd probably bruise. A second later she came, the first spasm so intense she almost knocked them both off the couch. He followed, pushing and pulsing inside her, the feral sound that ripped from his throat forever etched in her memory.

He was careful not to just collapse on top of her. But he held her in his arms as they made their way back to breathing, stopping for gentle kisses and lightly trailing fingers. She lay back and closed her eyes. Matt, everything, had been so much better than her dreams.

AN HOUR LATER THE SUN had moved and no longer warmed the couch. The air was probably chilly, but they weren't cold, not with the way Rachel's body was half draped over Matt.

"If I'd known back then," he said, lazy with contentment and the pure pleasure of being able to brush his palm over her skin. "That it would be like this, I would have brought you up here ten years ago."

"You liar. You were too afraid of me."

"True," he admitted, laughing. "You were a brazen little thing at Mill Creek."

"Hey."

"You're gonna deny that?" He rubbed the pad of his thumb back and forth over her puckered nipple.

"No." She almost left it at that, the flush surging up her chest distracting her, but then added, "I liked teasing you."

"You were a tease, all right. But the truth is, if I had acted on your advances, you would've run the other way."

"Probably. Only in the beginning."

He dragged his splayed hand up to her throat, then slipped around to her nape, the curl of his fingers exerting just the right amount of pressure to make her hold her breath as he pulled her mouth to his.

"Once I almost called your bluff," he whispered, then only tasted and taunted with his tongue and teeth, when she'd expected total devastation.

"When?"

"The time Wallace nearly caught us."

It took a moment for her foggy brain to recall the incident. Matt had been repairing the irrigation system near the short strip of jutting land where the Sundance bordered the Lone Wolf. She'd ridden Sylvie, a young bay mare, to look for him. He was working shirtless, and the sight of his tanned sweaty body had sent her newly awakened hormones somersaulting.

God, she'd been particularly shameless that day, stripping down to her bikini, strutting around, trying to get him to follow her to Mill Creek. Sex hadn't been the goal. She'd been too young and a little afraid to fantasize beyond kissing. The brazenness was only possible because she'd known she was safe with Matt.

"I remember," she said, her lashes fluttering closed when his mouth moved to her ear, the friction of his thumb rubbing her nipple becoming almost unbearable. "We heard his fourwheeler just in time."

Matt drew back, his breath washing over her earlobe. His hand stilled. "Man, I was tempted...."

She wished he hadn't stopped, though the intriguing gleam in his eyes aroused her curiosity. "To follow me?"

"To let the old man catch us." His smile was different, kind of unpleasant. "Wouldn't you have loved to have seen his face?"

"Not really." She shifted away, but Matt barely noticed.

He stared past her out the window. "Everything was about work. He pushed and pushed, never considering I had it in me to defy him. Can you picture him finding me with a McAllister?" He snorted. "He would've had a heart attack on the spot and saved Mom and me a lot of trouble."

Rachel's stomach roiled. A bitter taste coated her mouth. She rose in search of her clothes, sickened by the hostile expression on Matt's face. She could've lived her whole life without seeing that dark side of him. If he thought his hatred for Wallace was gone, he was very mistaken.

So what were they doing here? What part did she play? Was Matt grabbing his last chance to stick it to his father? She slipped on her bra and fastened the clasp, then pulled on her panties and jeans.

"Rachel?" He was clearly startled, obviously too wrapped up in his own thoughts to notice she'd gathered her clothes. "What are you doing?" he asked, getting up and again slipping his hand behind her neck.

This time there would be no kiss. "I have to decorate for the dance tomorrow." She tugged her sweater over her head. "I told you, remember?"

"Right." He got into his briefs and jeans, then picked up his shirt and pulled it on, frowning as he buttoned it. "You okay?"

"I'm fine." She lifted her trapped hair from inside the neckline and draped it over her shoulder so she could put on her jacket. "A little chilly, but I'll live."

Subdued, he watched her step into her boots. Clearly he knew something was off. She only hoped he left it alone. "I expect the dance is still in the storage barn behind the hardware store," he said, and she nodded. "Can I help?"

"Jesse, Trace and a few others volunteered to set up the tables, chairs and stage."

"Volunteered?"

She smiled. "I didn't twist hard enough to break any bones."

Regret in his eyes, he stared at her for a long tense moment. "I shouldn't have brought up Wallace. That was stupid."

"He's bound to be on your mind today." She needed to remember that herself. This wasn't an easy time for Matt. And even if he had once considered using her to get back at his father, it didn't mean he hadn't cared for her. Or else he would've ignored her age and had sex with her.

The mood had dipped, though, and they didn't talk much on the drive back to the Sundance. He dropped her off, no kiss, or even an attempt made by either of them. But then that would've been risky. Rachel didn't need everyone knowing her business.

Since Nikki wasn't back yet, Matt didn't get out of the truck. She closed the passenger door, resigned that things would be left up in the air between them, but then he let down the power window. "What time you headed to town?" he asked.

"Not for a while. I have things to do here before I leave."

"I'd give you a ride, but I don't know when I'll get to talk to Nikki."

"Don't worry about it, really. I'll drive myself, or go with Trace to make sure he doesn't flake out on me."

His absent nod told her he was still juggling things in his head. "I'll show up at some point." He waited, his gaze sharpening as he studied her face. "If it's okay."

"Of course it is, but I'm putting you to work."

He seemed to relax, giving her a lopsided smile. "I figured as much."

"Maybe Nikki will want to come, too."

"Yeah," he said, lacking enthusiasm.

"It's your call mentioning it. After you two talk she may not want to be around people, or maybe putting up cheesy decorations would be a good distraction."

The preoccupied glaze to his eyes was back as he stared toward the house. "She likes hanging with you and Jamie. The thing is though—" he returned his gaze to her face "—I was hoping you and I could still get together afterward."

She should've been jumping for joy and ready to rescind her offer to help decorate. But the knot in her stomach from earlier hadn't quite disappeared. "I have a question," she said, unable to help herself, even knowing it was a bad idea. "Was I a rebellion for you?"

His unwavering gaze unnerved her. Perhaps because she'd been secretly hoping to catch him off balance. But he appeared to be a man who'd already given the question some thought. "Funny you should bring that up. I've been wondering if you feel that way about me."

12

RACHEL RAN LATE THE REST of the afternoon. Too many guest issues pulled her in several directions. Any other time she'd have sworn the dude ranch idea had been her dumbest yet. Today she welcomed other people's problems sidelining her own worries and head games.

She stopped at the second-floor landing, closing her eyes, convinced she could still feel the press of his lips on hers. How had he known just where to touch her? Or how much pressure to use? How could he possibly have known that looking deep into her eyes while she climaxed was the perfect thing to do?

With a start, she opened her eyes, glanced over the railing toward the living room, then hurried down the stairs.

Dwelling on Matt was not in her best interest. Not today, not any day. Yes, she cherished those times they'd spent at Mill Creek and sneaking out to meet him after dark. But they were different people now. Why had she presumed she still knew him? Why on earth could she imagine, even now, that she'd ever truly known him at all? She'd been sixteen, for pity's sake. Her biggest fear her junior year had been getting caught wearing the same blue sundress as Mary-Jane Ledet again.

After that fateful summer dance, Rachel would've died a slow death before confessing to her mother that the permanent grape juice stain had been intentional. Mary-Jane was a senior and had much bigger boobs. She'd made Rachel look as if she'd rummaged in her mom's closet for a dress she couldn't fill out.

It had been awful, a huge deal, full of teen angst. Even though Matt had left months earlier, and Rachel had already decided her life was over. Obviously that hadn't been the case. She was still very much alive and going as crazy as ever, trying to figure out the crack he'd made about his being her rebellion. The smart thing would be to let it go. He was leaving again, if not tomorrow, perhaps the day after. Which meant she really needed to avoid getting carried away.

She looked out the window, saw Jesse sitting in his truck and grabbed her jacket and purse. She didn't need him ditching her, too. Trace had gotten tired of waiting and left for town without her.

"When are you getting your own car?" Jesse asked, once they were on their way.

"You trying to tell me something?"

"Nope."

"Good." She sighed, letting her head fall back against the seat. "While you're gone to help Shea move can I use your truck?"

"Already planned on it." Jesse looked over at her. "What's wrong, Rach?"

"Nothing, it's just that…it used to be easy borrowing Mom's car because she never went anywhere. Lately she's either running to town or visiting her friends. It's great. I'm glad to see her have a life. But it's kinda weird, too, you know?"

"I wasn't talking about the car."

She turned to smile at her brother. She didn't have a favorite, and she trusted all of them with her life. But if she could tell anyone about the uncertainty she felt over her future, it was Jesse. A few months ago he'd been prepared to leave the

Sundance in order to help the family. He'd totally get why she felt compelled to stay.

"We don't have to talk if you don't want to," he said quietly.

Rachel laughed. "Afraid I'm going to dig deep?"

He smiled. "Come on, squirt, tell me what's going on."

"First, I'm so happy you have Shea, and that she's moving here. You guys are great together. Second, we don't have money for a car, so that's why I'm leeching off everyone else. And third…" She hesitated, took a breath. "I'm leaving once the Sundance gets back on track." He gave a small nod, and didn't react as if she were nuts. "I don't want to disappoint Mom, or you, or anyone else, but I want to work in the hotel industry."

"You'd do well in that business."

She waited. "That's it?"

"You're smart, organized and personable. I'm guessing one of the chains tried to recruit you already."

Rachel snorted. "Want to help me start packing? Or maybe get the door for me?"

Jesse just smiled, kept his eyes on the road. "Nobody, including me, wants you to go anywhere. But you didn't study for six years to mix margaritas every night."

"Okay, I get you're not surprised," she said. Jesse had been the first to go to college, then joined the air force and became a pilot. "Please tell me the whole family doesn't know."

"Nobody's said anything to me."

She bumped her head back against the seat a couple of times. Maybe she needed to loosen a few nuts and bolts. Nothing was working out today. "I'll give you a ride to the airport tomorrow. But only because you're leaving me your truck."

He raised his eyebrows at her. "What about Matt?"

"What about him?"

"How's it going between you two?"

"That's a weird question." She folded her arms across her chest. "Was it Trace? Is it about the casserole?"

"Since I have no idea what you're talking about, I'll take a stab at it and say no."

She'd heard the defensiveness in her own voice, recognized it in her body language and forced herself to relax. "Matt has a lot going on. You must know about Nikki by now," she said, and he nodded. "And Mr. Gunderson is, well, I'm sure Matt wouldn't mind my telling you…his father's terminal. But that stays here because I don't know if Matt's talked to Nikki yet."

"He told you first," Jesse said, frowning.

"She wasn't around when he came by earlier. What is the matter with you, anyway?"

"I like Matt. Always have. Hated the way Gunderson treated him. But you're my sister. I don't want to see you hurt."

"What?" She felt her face heating, which really pissed her off. "That's a completely ridiculous thing to say. Matt and I are friends."

"You can't expect him to be the same guy you knew ten years ago."

Well, hell, she'd gone over that in her head earlier today. She didn't want to hear it from Jesse, or anyone else. "You think because he's some hotshot rodeo star he's out to nail every woman he can? Including me?" she murmured, crossing her arms again. "Matt isn't like that."

Jesse exhaled slowly, the low sound of his breath getting on her nerves. She wasn't looking for anyone's input. "I agree," he said finally. "But the guy has fought his share of demons. Maybe he's worked it out by now. For both your sakes, I hope so."

Rachel stared at him, the churning in her belly not to be ignored. What did Jesse know that she didn't? Unless it was important he never would've broached the subject. Of her three brothers he was the most circumspect, the least likely to tread into her business. "I don't understand."

"I know you," he said, giving her a patient smile. "You've checked him out online."

"Well, yeah, of course I did, and there's a ton of stuff, but I'm still not following you."

"Did you go back to articles on his early career?"

"Some."

"He was pretty wild. Both in the arena and in his private life. He took a lot of unnecessary risks."

"I did see a blog to that effect, but he was younger and obviously he's on the right path now."

"He was lucky, because there was a definite pattern. More than one reporter noticed he seemed to have a death wish. He rode when he was hurt, was getting into bar fights…does that sound like Matt?"

She shook her head. "You've made your point," she said, and turned to stare out the window in silence.

The scars…so many…no wonder he'd been uneasy. She'd bet not all of the wounds *had* come with the territory. She wasn't disappointed to learn this about him or afraid that he'd irrevocably changed, because at his core he wasn't a man prone to violence. Somehow she understood that he'd felt he deserved the punishment. And that broke her heart.

Oh, crap, she should be used to it. Matt Gunderson had already broken her heart more than once. Sadly, she feared he wasn't done.

FIRST THING RACHEL DID when she arrived at the storage barn was open the windows and swing the doors wide, hoping to diffuse the scent of old hay and saddle soap. Clearly no one had remembered to ask Mr. Jorgensen to air the place out. But it would be fine…it wasn't as if the familiar smells would chase away partygoers.

Louise and Sylvia from the fabric shop showed up minutes later, as did the elderly Lemon sisters. And right behind them came Gretchen, who warned them she only had forty-five minutes before her shift started at the Watering Hole.

Trace's friend Sam, a nice-looking hand from the Circle K who'd moved to town two years ago, was helping reinforce the stage. Rachel had met him in the fall, then seen him around town on occasion. Sam had been worthy of a second and third look, but his problem was that he knew he was hot. So no thank you.

Everyone went straight to work, the women happily observing the unwritten rule that chatting and gossiping were requisites as they unpacked last year's decorations. Between loud strikes of the hammer, the men contributed muffled curses that the women ignored, or at least pretended to.

It was all very familiar and comforting for Rachel. The activity kept her mind occupied and made the time speed by, until the subject of Matt came up. She promptly excused herself from cutting strips of red crepe paper to find the thermos she'd set down somewhere.

Dammit, she didn't want to think about him. As if she could block the images of him from this afternoon, naked, aroused and utterly stunning. Even that wasn't her biggest problem. Reliving the gentle and sure way he'd touched her, remembering the tenderness in his eyes—that would be her undoing.

After peeking outside, disappointed she didn't see his truck, she pulled out the old wooden ladder from behind the loft steps. Had she been thinking clearly, she would've brought a more sturdy model from this century. But she wasn't going up that high, so she enlisted Miriam Lemon's help to hold the ladder steady, and then went to work hanging shiny red hearts from the rafters.

An hour later, she climbed down. Backing up while studying the spacing of the hearts, Rachel asked, "What do you think?"

No one answered so she turned to Miriam and her sister, Mabel, who stood sullenly to the side. The twins were eighty going on twelve. If you asked one of them to do something, you'd better come up with an equally important task for the other.

"Oh?" Mabel pursed her pale wrinkled lips, faking surprise. "Were you asking for my opinion?"

Rachel sighed. "Anybody feel free to speak up."

The second the two women started talking over each other, Rachel realized her mistake. They thought the hearts should be evenly hung and not falling to different heights. Everyone knew valentine hearts were red, so why were some silver and pink? And should someone stand guard over the punch bowl tomorrow night to keep hellions from adding spirits?

At the back of the barn, Jesse and Sam were hooking up additional lighting, both clearly aware of the Pandora's box she'd opened. She was pretty sure electrical work hadn't plastered the grins on their faces.

The twins moved on to discuss the merits of the band that had been chosen for the dance. The members attended the high school, and according to the sisters, it was no secret that kids nowadays were incapable of recognizing good music.

Rachel tried to tune them out. She doubted they noticed her absence when she returned the ladder. Or perhaps they had, because their voices grew louder, following her around the large barn while she picked up boxes and trash and inspected the sturdiness of the folding tables that still needed to be set up.

God help her, she was not in the mood for this nonsense. She thought Jamie and Nikki might have shown up by now, and Jesse's warning lurked somewhere in her brain, nagging at her.

The thermos was empty, and she grabbed it, hoping to get a refill at the Watering Hole or Marge's Diner. If nothing else, the walk would do her good. She needed the fresh air and solitude, a few private minutes to let her own thoughts drive her insane. Why should the sisters have all the fun?

Oh, yeah, she was losing it, all right. She breathed the brisk air deep into her lungs. To the west, pale pink remnants of the sun wove through the Belt Mountains. No snow was forecast, which made her happy. For the sake of the dance and herself. She'd hate having to rearrange activities for the Sundance guests tomorrow.

Darkness was gathering quickly over the town, sending most people home for supper. Several trucks and cars were parked outside the diner, a few more pickups hugged the curb in front of the Watering Hole down the block. For a second she thought she spotted Nikki on the sidewalk near the bar but a huge customized truck with obnoxiously big tires blocked her view.

She looked both ways, then started to cross Main when she got another glimpse. It was Nikki, talking to the husky kid that had hired on at the Lone Wolf last fall—the bodyguard. Rachel didn't know his real name, but everyone used the moniker behind his back because he clearly spent too much time pumping iron and rarely left Gunderson's side.

A friend had shown up with him one day—she'd heard his name was Tony—stocky, but not as muscular, or much past the legal age. Both wore tough-guy expressions, Stetsons and boots like uniforms. But neither were cowboys. She'd have to remember to ask Matt about them. And what the hell was Nikki doing with the bodyguard? He wasn't her type.

Rachel got her answer when Nikki hauled off and slapped him across the face. He laughed and grabbed her wrist. She yelled at him, then used her free hand to slap him again. Her palm connected with his cheek in a wallop that echoed off the bar's brick facade. His head flew to the side.

Shocked, Rachel froze for a moment, still too far to help. But she found her feet quickly when she saw the anger explode in the man's face.

"Get the hell away from her," Rachel shouted, dropping the thermos and running toward them.

The man didn't even spare her a glance. He caught Nikki's

other wrist and twisted. She cried out, cursed a blue streak and tried to knee him. Loud country music spilled out of the bar onto the street. It was likely Nikki and Rachel had gone unheard.

She had to get help from inside the Watering Hole. Before she could, Matt's pickup jammed to a screeching halt in the middle of the street. He jumped out and charged the man. Either the guy was taken by surprise or the blind fury in Matt's face convinced him to release Nikki. She stumbled backward, saved from hitting the sidewalk by the brick wall. On impact she gasped.

"You son of a bitch." Matt grabbed the front of the shorter man's shirt and dragged his face up to his. In a low and deadly voice, he said, "Touch her again and I'll kill you."

"Screw you, Gunderson. You and your big-shot attitude. You don't scare me."

Matt's free hand balled into a fist that shook with restraint. Veins popped from his neck and forehead. Rachel had never seen him so enraged.

"Forget it, Matt." Nikki touched his arm. "Let him go. The jerk's not worth it."

Matt wouldn't take his piercing gaze off the other man's face, wouldn't release his shirt.

"See?" The guy winked at Nikki. "She liked it."

Nikki hung on to Matt's arm. If she hadn't, Rachel was certain he would've taken a swing.

She saw the fire raging in his eyes, and frightened for him, she moved closer. "Matt, don't. He's goading you into taking the first punch."

"Listen to her," Nikki pleaded.

The bodyguard turned to eye Rachel, his boozy breath assaulting her. "Wouldn't mind a taste of you either."

She reared her head in disgust, saw the control slip from Matt. He tried to shake Nikki off, but her persistence ended up leaving him vulnerable. The bodyguard's beefy fist slammed into Matt's face. He staggered back, landing against his sister.

The Watering Hole door opened with a blast of music.

Rachel turned, desperate for help to stop the fight.

"Eddie, what's going on?" It was the friend, Wallace's other thug.

The momentary disruption allowed Matt to recover. He went after Eddie, throwing a punch that clipped his jaw and knocked him to the sidewalk.

Tony didn't hesitate. Leaving his buddy on the ground, he rushed Matt.

"Stop it, please. Stop!" Rachel tried to throw herself between them, but Matt yanked her out of the way.

Again he paid for the interference, suffering a thudding blow to his gut. Rachel exchanged a helpless glance with Nikki. Matt was outnumbered, and the men looked as if they wanted to beat the hell out of him.

Eddie had jumped to his feet. Rachel and Nikki tried to block him from ganging up on Matt. He shoved them aside as if they were nothing but rag dolls, and Rachel fell to the sidewalk. The experience stunned her. To be roughly handled like that by a man shook her to her core. Nikki recovered immediately. She grabbed a two-by-four from the bed of a parked pickup, while Rachel watched in mute horror as the two men pounded Matt with their fists.

He threw his fair share of punches, bloodying Eddie's face, then landing a blow that temporarily doubled Tony over. But with two of them on him, Matt didn't stand much of a chance. The confusion also prevented Nikki from taking a clear swing without clipping her brother.

Rachel forced her feet to move. Someone in the Watering Hole would help. She thought she heard Trace yelling from a distance and turned around. He was running toward them. But it was too late to save Matt from hitting the ground.

Tony kicked him in the stomach. Matt curled into himself, using his arm to protect his ribs and avoiding the toe of Eddie's boot. Seizing her chance, Nikki smashed the two-by-four across Eddie's back. With a yelp of pain, he fell to his knees.

Time seemed to freeze. Tony glared at Nikki, but he didn't seem anxious to strike a woman. "Put it down," he growled at her.

"Screw you." She lifted it higher. "Stay away from my brother."

He jerked in obvious surprise, then frowned at Matt.

"You stupid bitch," Eddie muttered, one hand holding his back, while using the other to push himself up.

"Call me that again, I'll take your goddamn head off." Nikki's hands shook, but she tightened her grip.

Matt almost made it to his feet, but Tony kicked him again.

"Tony, listen." Rachel moved in, holding a restraining hand out to Nikki. "Your friend started this fight," Rachel said, hoping her instinct was right about the younger man. She glanced down at Matt, knowing she had to stop this peacefully. He was in a rage and wanted an outlet, no matter what the odds. "Eddie grabbed Nikki. She tried to get away. Matt was protecting her. I saw everything."

Confusion creased Tony's face. He didn't automatically leap to his friend's defense. Nor did he interfere when Matt slowly stood. In fact, the suspicious look Tony pinned on Eddie gave Rachel hope this would end here.

Struggling to his feet, Eddie cursed viciously. "She was asking for it."

Matt swore and would've lunged for him, but Nikki cut him off by placing herself between the men.

"Jesus, Eddie," Tony said, shaking his head.

"You're not gonna back me up?" He glared in disbelief at his friend before turning to rush Matt, who seemed ready to oblige.

Luckily, Trace had finally reached them.

Unfortunately, it was Tony he punched.

In seconds, fists were flying. Rachel and Nikki screamed in unison for everyone to stop. A pair of Circle K wranglers coming out of the bar, and Jesse, brought the brawl to a halt.

No encouragement required, Tony and Eddie jumped in their red Dodge Ram and sped down Main Street. A deputy—had to be Roy—driving the sheriff's truck, passed the Dodge as he entered the town limits. He'd eventually notice them clustered outside the Watering Hole, if he hadn't already.

"What do you think?" Jesse glanced from the slowing pickup to Matt, who used his sleeve to wipe the blood from his chin.

"No use getting him involved. Those bastards will get their asses fired tomorrow." He looked at Nikki. "Unless you want to press—"

"No." She shook her head, stared unblinkingly after the men, her hands still clutching the two-by-four like a lifeline.

"You were awesome," Rachel said, feeling ashamed over her reaction to being shoved. "Really quick thinking."

Nikki let out a faint whimper that seemed to embarrass her.

"You were." Trace gently loosened the piece of wood from her grasp. "You were amazing."

Her shocked gaze flicked to his face, sharpened when it touched on the small cut on his lower lip and then flitted away. She straightened her spine and slid her fingers through her hair. "I need a drink. Matt, you?"

"I'm gonna pass." He tried to hide his wince, but Rachel saw it and noticed his right arm discreetly pressed to his ribs.

"You're hurt," she said, feeling like an idiot. He'd been kicked in the stomach, for God's sake.

He shrugged, probing his battered face. "Yeah, I'll probably have a shiner, but this is nothing."

"Bull." Nikki's worried dark eyes widened as if she were really seeing him for the first time after the fight.

"You're seeing Dr. Heaton." Rachel slid an arm around him.

"The hell I am," he argued, and slumped against her.

13

"GOD, MATT, RACHEL's right—you have to see the doctor." Nikki had rushed to his other side, her expression stricken.

"I'm not hurt bad enough," he said irritably. "You've seen me worse off." With a quiet grunt, he forced himself to stand straighter, and slanted Rachel a look. "I meant from competing. Not fighting."

"I got that." She held him tighter, noticed the bruising and swelling that had started to mar his handsome features. "It's still a good idea to let the doctor have a look."

"I'll think about it. Right now I'd like to get off the sidewalk." He squinted at Roy climbing out of the sheriff's vehicle now parked behind Matt's. "My truck still running?"

"I cut the engine," Jesse said. "I'll move it closer." He turned to the wranglers who'd helped break up the fight and the others who had trickled out of the bar when they'd finally heard the commotion. "Everybody go on back into the Watering Hole."

There was nodding and shuffling, and then the crowd was gone. Jesse headed toward Matt's truck, stopping to talk with Roy. Trace stuck close, his hands jammed in his pockets. Rachel knew he was still tense and pumped full of adrenaline. She hoped he wasn't planning on doing something stupid.

"I'm so sorry, Matt." Nikki stared at his scraped chin, her eyes moist, but no tears fell. "This was my fault."

"Hell, Nik, none of this is your fault." Matt pulled away from her to look into her face. "Did you want him to touch you?"

"No." The word flew out in a shaky whoosh. "I told him to get away or I'd kick him in the—" She sighed. "I guess trouble will always follow me," she murmured to herself. "I just wish you hadn't gotten involved. You know I can take care of myself."

"Ah, Nik." He rubbed her arm, and Rachel looked away from the private moment. Something told her they'd had a similar conversation before.

She ached for them both. Nikki obviously had demons of her own, and poor Matt…he wanted to be that big brother who made everything better, but he was damaged, too. God, how Rachel hated Wallace Gunderson at this moment. She didn't care that he was dying. Maybe with him gone his children could have some peace.

"I'm going to take care of you, Matt," Nikki said, using her thumb to wipe the blood from the corner of his mouth. "We'll clean you up, maybe call the doctor, huh? Just to be sure."

Matt sighed, briefly closing his eyes.

Rachel's whole body tensed. She couldn't walk away now. She wanted to take care of him. Of course she understood Nikki wanted to be with her brother, but Rachel had to do this. Needed this.

"Hey, Nikki." Trace waited for her to meet his eyes. "I think Rachel will take really good care of Matt."

Nikki blinked, turned to look at her brother and then to Rachel. The torn expression on the younger woman's face tugged at Rachel's heart, but she couldn't find it inside to be charitable about this. Matt was hers. Just for tonight.

A strained smile curved Nikki's lips. "Matt?"

"Go have a drink with Trace. In fact, have one for me, too."

She seemed uncertain, but then reluctantly nodded.

Trace finger-combed his hair. "Look here." He probed the corner of his mouth. "I cut my lip. If you're offering TLC I could use some."

Rachel laughed.

Nikki rolled her eyes. "I'll buy you a shot."

He gave her the trademark grin that had gotten him in and out of trouble since he was twelve. "Well, darlin', now you're talking."

"What?" Nikki said dryly. "You forgot my name already?"

At that, Matt laughed. It ended in a groan. "I'm okay," he said, putting up a hand, his glare daring anyone to contradict him. "Go," he ordered when uncertainty reappeared on Nikki's face. "So I can get off my feet."

"Fine," she said with a snap in her voice and headed for the Watering Hole door.

Trace mouthed that he'd take her back to the Sundance, and followed her into the bar.

Matt watched them go. "Those two ever get together I don't know which one to feel sorrier for."

Rachel adjusted her hold around his waist. "Let's worry about taking care of you."

"Did you drive, or shall we take my truck?"

Jesse walked up to them. "I told Roy you'd call him if you or Nikki wanted to give a statement. No one will bother you tonight." He finished fiddling with his key chain and held up a key. "Noah is out of town. Use his guest room. His place is just around the corner," Jesse said for Matt's benefit.

Rachel frowned, at first not sure what to say, then finally asked, "Did Roy give that to you?"

"He offered, because he knew Noah wouldn't mind. But I have my own key. Cole and I each have one," he said, studying her face as if he could somehow communicate something without spelling it out. "From a while back, okay?"

"But—"

"Rachel, take the key." Jesse dropped it in her palm. "Matt will explain it to you later." The men exchanged smiles, then Jesse strode down Main Street.

She stared after him for a moment. Why wasn't she getting this? Switching her gaze to the key nestled in her palm, she wondered if Jesse had changed his mind about Matt since their ride into town, or if he'd simply chosen to trust her instincts.

Sighing, she glanced at the door to the Watering Hole. Trace would see to Nikki. Jesse would smooth things over if Rachel didn't go home tonight.

"We'll take your truck," she said, pocketing the key and looking at Matt. God, his poor face.

"He said Noah lives around the corner."

"Right, but I'm not going to let you walk."

"You're making too big a deal out of this."

"Tough." She guided him to the curb where Jesse had parked the pickup.

He leaned heavily on her, but he didn't seem to have trouble walking. "This sucks, tomorrow night being the dance and all."

"You don't dance anyway."

Matt snorted. "How do you know I haven't learned?"

She opened the passenger door. "Have you?"

"No, but at least I'm not too embarrassed to shuffle my feet and pretend."

Rachel smiled. "Let's make you better first. Get in."

"I can drive."

"Dammit, Matthew."

Sighing, he held the door for support and slowly straightened to slide onto the seat.

"It's your ribs, isn't it?" she asked. "And don't lie."

"Yeah, but they're just bruised." He paused to settle in. "I'm not being stupid or trying to be macho. I have to be in shape to ride in two weeks."

She hated the idea of him climbing on a bull that soon, but just nodded. "I think we should stop at the sheriff's office and get a first aid kit from Roy."

"I have one stowed in the back with everything we need."

She closed the door, then went around to the driver's side. Good for him for being responsible and carrying his own kit. Too bad it made her think of Jesse's earlier warning, and she had to bite her lip to keep from asking Matt if he used it often.

The drive took three minutes. Another two to navigate the narrow sidewalk to the small house and unlock the front door.

"Noah has a white picket fence." Matt chuckled, walking over the threshold without her help. The house was old, the doorway narrow. "Who'd have thunk it?"

"The place belongs to the county." Rachel flipped a wall switch that turned on a pair of brass lamps flanking a tan leather couch. "It's part of his compensation package."

"I'm still gonna give him shit over it."

Rachel found that oddly reassuring and smiled. "I've never been here before," she said, glancing around the room designed for comfort and not style. The recliner was worn, the wooden floors in need of refinishing, and the stone fireplace was big enough to heat the entire house. "Why don't you sit while I find the bathroom and set up."

"Set up?" He touched his cheek and chin, then checked his fingers. "I'm not bleeding anymore. I need a damp paper towel, cotton balls and a tube of NEOSPORIN. That's it."

"And your ribs?"

He gave her a crooked smile. "See? Told you it's nothing. I forgot already."

"Stop looking adorable. I won't let it distract me." She surveyed the painful-looking scrape on his cheek from being pummeled to the sidewalk, then ran her gaze down the front of his black-and-gray flannel shirt. Blood stained his collar and his sleeve was torn. "Will you sit?"

"No, let's get this over with."

Carrying the first aid kit, she led him down the hall. She noticed what had to be the guest room on the right. A double bed covered with a navy-and-brown patchwork quilt was the only furniture in the small room. Off to the left was the bathroom, a very tiny bathroom with ugly turquoise walls and a dated tub and sink. She put down the toilet seat cover, then stepped aside for him to sit while she got rid of her jacket.

He'd already started unbuttoning his shirt and had pulled the hem from his jeans. Standing in the doorway, he paused to probe his ribs. His fingers were slow and careful like a man who'd done this many times. When he finally looked up, the relief in his eyes was genuine. "Yeah, they're just bruised."

"I hope so." She watched him bypass the sink, amused that he hadn't even glanced in the mirror. Wow, not her...that would've been the first thing she'd done. "You'll have to take off your shirt."

"Right." He grimaced with the effort, and she slipped between him and the tub to help.

She hung the shirt on the side of the tub and bent to open the first aid kit sitting on the floor. Finding a soft sterile cloth sealed in plastic and everything else she needed, she straightened and looked at him, her heart fluttering.

"I'm sorry you have to see me like this," he said, his eyes bleak. "But thank you."

"All I see is a man who defended his sister. Though I wouldn't have expected anything less from you."

"Don't do it." He slumped back, his expression guarded. "Don't expect anything of me or you'll end up disappointed."

Rachel turned to the sink to wet the cloth, not wanting him to see that his remark had hurt her. "I'm not looking for a relationship, Matt," she said, her words a bit more clipped than she'd intended. "You can stop worrying."

"No." He caught her arm and pulled her to stand between

his spread legs. "You have it wrong," he said, looking into her eyes. "It's not you—it's me. I'll disappoint you."

"Because you think I want something, but I don't."

"Christ, Rachel, I know I have nothing you want. I also don't have a history of meeting expectations. You, if anyone, should understand that."

She didn't like the "have nothing you want" phrasing, especially stated so matter-of-factly. "I'm not following." She gently touched the cloth to his cheek. "Are you talking about Wallace? Why does he suddenly count? Nothing you could've done would please him, and only because he knew you were the better man. Even as a teenager, you were the better man."

His head tipped slightly back, Matt's reluctant smile slid into a wince when she dabbed the cloth around the gash on his jaw. She knew it stung, hated that she hurt him, but there was no other choice. The wounds had to be cleaned.

"If I did anything right it was because of you, Rachel. You saw the best in me. Whenever I started to lose my temper I'd picture your face, imagine you were there watching me, and what would you think if I'd hauled off and flattened Wallace."

"You give me too much credit." She gave him a wry smile before rinsing the cloth. "I might've cheered you on."

He put a hand on her hip, held still while she went back to work. "You would've told me it wasn't worth it and to walk away."

She lifted her shoulder in a small shrug. "Today, yes. Back when I was sixteen, I don't know." Sighing, she avoided his gaze. "Though tonight I managed to surprise myself." She cleared her throat and focused on his chin. "Worse, I humiliated myself."

He moved his head back. "How?"

Balling the cloth and setting it on the sink, she was in no hurry to meet his eyes. "I froze. I'm usually good in an emergency… I am. But when Eddie shoved me, I was so startled I froze. Not Nikki, she was great. She—"

"Don't compare yourself to her. Nik's lived in rough neighborhoods most of her life. She's a scrapper and had to be to survive. You have no reason to be embarrassed."

"But you needed me…they had you down on the ground and if I hadn't hesitated maybe—"

"Look at me." He waited, but she stubbornly stared down at the NEOSPORIN cap she was unscrewing. He nudged up her chin until his troubled eyes captured hers. "These scars on my body…most of them are hazards of the job. But not all of them. I was angry and full of hatred toward Wallace, myself, and I even resented my mom sometimes because she wouldn't leave him. I got into bar fights, not giving a damn about anything other than an excuse to hit someone." A muscle worked in his jaw. "I thought I'd worked out my anger issues. Tonight, when I saw him touch Nikki, I was furious. But I managed to keep my cool. When he shoved you, I was that guy again. I wanted to kill him with my bare hands. If I hadn't been down, I don't know what I would've done."

Rachel smiled and squeezed some ointment on her fingertips. "You would've stopped yourself."

"I don't know that. Neither do you."

She did, but she wouldn't argue. Hell, she'd wanted to string the guy up, too. "After I finish applying this salve I'm going to get some ice. It'll help keep the swelling down."

He nodded, said nothing, just watched her.

Apparently Noah didn't believe in frozen vegetables. He had no peas or anything else to use as a compress, so she found a plastic bag and filled it with ice. On her way back to Matt, she glanced into the guest room again, noted the perfectly made bed, and it finally occurred to her why Noah had given her brothers keys to his place. She reentered the bathroom, chuckling at herself for being dense.

Matt smiled. "What did I miss?"

"Nothing, really. Just—" She folded the bag of ice in a dry towel and pressed it gently to the swelling near his eye. "Should we wrap your ribs?"

He cupped his palm over the ice pack. "Nope. Not for bruising. Tell me what the joke was."

She studied his chest, glad that Noah had a big ice dispenser because they were going to need a second bag. "The keys Noah gave Jesse and Cole. I finally got it." She couldn't hold herself back from brushing her fingertips over the already-darkening skin.

"This part I like," he said, his warm moist breath bathing her ear and the side of her neck. "What about the key thing?"

"Is this a test?" She gave him an eye roll and kept petting him, careful not to press hard.

"I'm not sure *I* got it." His smile told her that was crap, but then he grunted and jerked.

"I'm sorry. I'll stop."

"No, don't. It was just that one spot."

"You sure?"

"I'll let you know when I'm uncomfortable." He skimmed her waist and hip with his free hand.

She let her palm rest over his heart for just a moment, then smiled as she leaned back. "Is there anyplace else that hurts?" She brushed aside the hair falling across his forehead, and checked for more scrapes or bruises.

"None. Quit stalling."

"Noah gave them the key so they could bring women here. Happy?" She made a face. "Living at the Sundance is like being in the middle of a state fair." She crouched to drop the NEO-SPORIN in the first aid kit and closed it. "Huh. Jesse didn't say anything about Trace having his own key." She laughed. "I wouldn't have given him one either." She rose, bringing the box with her. "I shouldn't say that. I like teasing him but it's not his fault women are stupid around him. And he doesn't take advantage of—"

Matt took the kit from her and tried to balance it on the edge of the small sink since there was no counter to speak of. The plastic box tilted and partially landed inside the sink. He ignored it and took her hands in his.

"Where's your ice pack?" she asked, her heart starting to pound when she looked into his darkened eyes. He was hurt. Surely that was pain, not lust. Not so soon after the fight.

"You think that's why Jesse gave you his key? Because he knew we needed privacy?"

"Jesse knew you were hurt and, therefore, harmless."

Matt almost smiled at that. "I doubt it," he said, letting go of her hands.

But before she could draw back, he slid his arms around her waist and pulled her more snugly between his spread legs. "This is crazy," she murmured. "You'll do more damage to—" She cut herself off when he pressed his uninjured cheek to her breasts.

"We'll have to be careful," he said, sliding a hand over the swell of her backside.

"How can you even think about sex right now?"

"Honey, I haven't stopped thinking about it since I saw you the first night." He turned his head and, through her worn college sweatshirt, sought her nipple. "You have to take this off."

"Matt, you can't do this." She picked up the ice pack he'd left on the shelf behind him.

He pushed his hand under the sweatshirt and smiled up at her. "I plan on making you do all the work."

Rachel's laugh came out an inelegant snort. She pretended to cough. "Will you please keep this compress on for a while?"

"Sure, for as long as it takes you to turn down the guest-room bed."

She took in the scrapes on his cheek and chin, the swelling and bruising around his eye. "I don't believe this."

"We'll keep the lights off," he said grimly.

"That's not what I meant. God, Matt." She leaned down to gently brush a kiss to his mouth. Except for the small cut at the corner, his lips weren't too bad. "Tonight you rest. Tomorrow we'll renegotiate."

Sighing, he withdrew his hand from under her sweatshirt and took the ice pack. "You know where the guest room is?"

"We passed it in the hall." She took his arm to help him up, but he said, "Thanks, I'm good."

She moved back and let him stand on his own. He didn't seem to struggle, though he didn't hurry either. Dammit, she hoped she wasn't making a mistake by not calling Dr. Heaton. Yet Matt was a grown man, and he should know if he needed medical care.

"You all right?" she asked, unable to help herself.

"To be honest, better than I initially thought. Lead the way."

"No, you first."

He smiled. "So you can catch me if I fall?"

"Exactly right."

"I'm not going to fall, Rachel," he said, but let her follow.

As soon as they entered the room she got busy pulling down the quilt and sheets. She fluffed the pillows, then hovered as he lowered himself to the edge of the bed.

"I'll get you some water then clean up the bathroom—" She gasped when he caught her wrist.

"That can wait." He pulled her down to the bed beside him.

She didn't resist for fear of injuring him. "Matt, we just agreed that tomorrow—"

"I didn't agree to a damn thing," he said and kissed her.

14

"THIS IS SO FOOLISH," Rachel murmured against his mouth, ashamed of herself because she should be firmer, and not let him pull up her sweatshirt and unclasp her bra. "Matt."

He took advantage of her open mouth and slipped his tongue inside, then pushed aside her loosened bra cups and palmed her breasts.

She let him kiss her, telling herself that to do otherwise could inflict harm, but she knew better. She didn't want him to stop.

When Matt finally tore his mouth away from hers, she felt relieved and bereft at the same time. "Help a cowboy out and take off your clothes," he said, his lips lifting in a slow sexy smile designed to get his way. The coaxing hand he slid up her thigh was either backup or a distraction.

She shifted, angling her legs away from him, because one more inch and she'd be unable to think clearly. Not that she was doing a bang-up job of it now. "I suppose you want help with your jeans and boots, too."

His smile broadened. "I'd be mighty grateful."

"Oh, brother, don't lay it on too thick." She got to her feet, hoping he didn't notice the shuddering breath that trembled through her body.

"No," he said, when she went for his boots. "You strip first."

"Strip?" She laughed. "What, you want a little dance action, too?"

He shook his head, his eyes locked on her, humor absent from his face. "I want to see you naked again. This afternoon was—I haven't been able to stop thinking about you."

"Me, too," she admitted, need for him swelling in her chest. "I'll never forget today. Never."

His brows drew together in a troubled frown. "No regrets?"

"God, no."

He relaxed. "I wish we were in Kalispell right now. I'd keep you in bed for a week."

"That would be okay with me."

"Come on, take your clothes off. I'm not going first. Don't want you leaving me in my boxers and running out on me."

"I'm not running out on you, Matt," she said, and when he flinched, she realized she'd hit a nerve. She hadn't meant anything, but apologizing seemed pointless.

She unlaced and toed off her running shoes, unzipped and unsnapped her jeans, then shimmied out of them. Her pink bikini panties stayed right where they were while she pulled the sweatshirt over her head and tossed it. The unfastened bra hung uselessly, and moving back her shoulders, she let it fall down her back to the floor.

Matt watched her with an intensity that made her mouth dry. The tip of his tongue slipped out and touched his lower lip. Scrapes, bruises, nothing could detract from the sexy expression of want on his face.

With shaky hands, she crouched before him and managed to pull off his boots and socks. He threaded a hand through her hair, refusing to let go when she pushed to her feet. But when she reached around him to stack the pillows against the headboard, he switched to her breast, plucking at her nipple and then brushing featherlight strokes with his thumb.

She arched into his touch, and giving up any illusion of self-control, she leaned in, her lips parted for him. His tongue slid inside and moved deep into her mouth. She was already damp between her thighs, her breath shallow. Another second and she'd refuse him nothing.

Dragging her mouth away, she straightened and inched back out of his reach. He looked at her as if she'd slapped him. "Can you swing your legs onto the bed, or do you need help?"

"Rachel—"

"Look, I'm just trying to get you comfortable first."

His gaze fell to her lips, then to her breasts. He slowly brought one leg up, scooted his butt toward the headboard and lifted the other leg onto the bed, already unfastening his jeans. He drew down the zipper and hooked his thumbs in the waistband. "You'll have to help me pull these off."

She had to kneel on the bed to do the job smoothly. He lifted his upper back off the mattress, propping himself up with his elbows and watched her. Hard to believe that was the most comfortable position for his bruised ribs. Resisting the impulse to point that out, she used her energy to rid him of the jeans. Leaving him half-hard in his boxers.

Forcing her gaze away, she slid off the bed to stash his jeans. There was no furniture. She dropped them on the floor next to hers. "How are you doing?"

"Better and better."

She recognized that wicked tone and looked at him. He was checking out her ass. "You have prescription pain pills in your first aid kit."

"They have to be about two years old."

"Probably still better than aspirin."

"I know what I need." His gaze slid down her body. "Come here."

"I'm serious, Matt," she said, one hand on her hip, able to stand her ground as long as he wasn't touching her.

"Hell, are you gonna make me climb out of bed?"

Rachel sighed. So much for staying firm. "I won't allow you to keep blackmailing me like this," she said, even as she crawled onto the mattress. "And it wouldn't kill you to take a pill. I promise it won't diminish your macho image."

He didn't smile or make a face, or do anything but continue to watch her. "I don't want anything in my system. Not now."

She stretched out beside him, lying on her side facing him. Was he worried about his performance? "Oh, Matt..."

He shifted, angling toward her, but not without wincing. Then he briefly brushed his lips across hers. "The panties have to go. But I can probably handle them."

"Maybe it's your head we should worry about, not your ribs. You're completely insane."

"Honey, that's not the part of my body I'm concerned with right now." He leaned over until his mouth rested on the curve between her neck and shoulder. The warmth of his breath made her shiver, but not half as much as the feel of his teeth scraping her skin gently, followed quickly by the wet hot slick of his tongue.

In spite of herself she arched toward him and bent her head to expose more of her neck to whatever wonderful thing he wanted to do. Her eyes drifted to half-mast and her sigh told him far too much about how she wanted him.

When the front of her thighs bumped his hard muscled ones, she lifted her lids, startled that she'd moved closer. She looked down, watched in a stupor, as he nibbled and licked his way down to her collarbone, his breath quickening as he meandered to her nipple.

She let her gaze run across his shoulders and arms, his poor banged-up middle, finally to his boxers. He was ridiculously hard, and she didn't get that at all because he still had to be in some pain.

"Are you okay?" she asked, gingerly touching his shoulder.

He paused, then flicked his tongue over the sensitive flesh. "You can't keep asking me that."

She pressed her lips together. "Promise to tell me if—"

He lifted his head. Their eyes met, briefly, then he glanced around the room. "Let's cut the overhead and use the hall light."

She hesitated, gently touching his face where she should've insisted he keep the ice. The swelling wasn't bad yet, but it would be.

He captured her hand and kissed her palm, then started to roll out of bed.

"No, I'll do it." She scrambled off her side, and turned off the switch.

"Close the door halfway."

"Your face isn't ruining the mood—it's knowing that you're hurting that's—"

He smiled a little.

"Okay, I'll shut up." Sighing, she slanted the door to redirect the light away from the bed. "Now lie back."

"Yes, ma'am." He eased his shoulders against the pillows, tracking her with his gaze, even in the dimness.

She went back to her side and slowly slid between the sheets.

"No covers," he said, motioning her closer.

"I'm cold."

"I'll take care of that."

She gave in because she could see he was ready to chase her across the mattress if she didn't move in beside him. "You know, a few more days until you felt better wouldn't kill us."

"I thought you were going to shut up." He turned, throwing an arm over her, and cutting off her protest with his mouth.

She kissed him back, her body quivering when he slid his hand down her belly and reached inside her panties. He deepened the kiss, a low frustrated moan coming from his throat when he could only jerk her panties partway down one hip.

She broke away to finish the job, coming up on her knees to take care of his boxers, as well.

Even in the dim glow of the hall light the sight of his arousal made her breath catch. She touched him, lightly trailing her fingertips along the smooth silky skin of his hard penis and then circling the tip.

Matt shuddered. "Come closer," he whispered, trying to reach for her.

"Tell me you have another condom."

"In my wallet. Back pocket of my jeans."

She really had to start thinking ahead. Again she scrambled off the bed, hastily found his jeans and took the brown leather billfold to him.

"Go ahead," he said, ignoring the extended wallet and cupping her breast instead.

She located two in a small hidden pocket and left the packets on the bed while she returned to exploring his aroused body. God, how much she wanted him. Inside her, filling her completely, his heat surging into her, the rough pads of his thumbs doing amazing things to her breasts. But not just that, she wanted him to look at her like he had before. She wanted to see his eyes fill with wonder as if she was the most precious gift he'd ever been given.

With a quiet grunt, Matt caught her right shoulder and forced her to lie back, then followed her down. He kissed the tip of her nose, her chin, and then lingered on the tingly skin below her ear. When he drew back, there it was, that wondrous look in his eyes that made her melt and left no doubt that for this moment he was completely hers.

He skimmed a hand from the base of her throat, over her breast and down her belly. When he discovered how wet she was, he breathed a deep sigh of satisfaction that shimmered through her entire body. His movements were slow, deliberate, erasing any fear that pain was in charge of this dance.

Rachel relaxed for the first time since she'd seen Nikki in front of the Watering Hole. Despite everything, he was gorgeous. Part of her wanted to turn on every light in the house so she could see the details, but this was perfect, too. Knowing no one was going to disturb them, seeing how much he wanted her.

She ran her hands down his back, his muscles twitching beneath her palm. The soft hiss of breath as she reached the upper curve of his behind was nice, but how he plunged two fingers inside her was even better.

Capturing her mouth again, he moaned as he thrust, mirroring the rhythm with his tongue, letting her know what he wanted to do next. She did her share of moaning, too, so afraid she was close to coming. She wanted to, very much, but not yet. Not until she…

When she squeezed his fingers, his gasp broke their kiss. The reaction made her even more eager to explore. Her hands skimmed his sides as she moved them up, then briefly let him go to grasp his shoulders.

Stilling his hand, he let out a surprised huff when she gently pushed him away. "What are you doing?"

"Everything," she said. "As soon as you're on your back."

The corner of his mouth quirked up. "Everything?"

"You'll never know if you don't do as you're asked."

"So bossy," he said, then frowned as he slipped his fingers out of her and lowered himself on the bed, but the stubborn mule pulled her down with him.

She was pressed against his side with his arm around her, and he was kissing her again. They got a little too enthusiastic before they both settled down to a wet, hot and slow tango.

Touching him was a study in self-control. With her thrumming heartbeat and the urgings of her more-than-ready body, she wanted to feel his strength and test those amazing muscles. Instead, she ran her fingertips gently down his body, all the way to his thick and eager erection.

"Oh, God." He groaned as if she were killing him instead of moving her hand around his shaft. He turned just enough on his side to capture her mouth with his own and run his hand down to her hip.

His hiss made her still her hand, certain he was moving too much, too fast.

"Dammit, Rachel," he said, his voice so deep and rough it gave her the shivers. "I don't give a damn about my ribs. I've ridden bulls in worse shape than this."

She looked up into his eyes, seeing the strain in his neck, in his shoulders. "What do you want?"

"You," he said, "in every way possible." Then he stole her breath in another overwhelming kiss, using his tongue and teeth and warm moist breath to drive her wild. When he finally pulled back, both of them desperate for air, he murmured, "Help me with the condom."

With a bit of searching, Rachel found the packets. She tucked one between the mattress and the box spring in case she needed it in a hurry. The other, she opened, and watched his face tense as she slipped it over him.

When she gripped him around the base, then moved her hand up until she could sweep her thumb over the head, his curses made her smile.

"If you care about me at all, you'll stop that right now," he said, his muscles tensing from his thighs to his neck.

She released him instantly. "Did I hurt you?"

He let go a long trembling breath. "No. I don't want to come yet."

She smiled as she moved back into position beside him, kissing whatever part of him she could on her way there.

"Have I told you how beautiful you are?" he said, lifting her chin so he could kiss her mouth.

Nothing extravagant this time. Just a sweet, gentle brush of lips and warm breath.

Blushing, she assumed he didn't want an answer. He'd told her earlier she was beautiful. Of course it was only pillow talk...but coming from Matt, she knew it was sincere.

"You are a stunner," he murmured, his eyes darkening. "If I could, I'd spend days and days showing you." He caressed her breast again, then straightened his hand and brushed her aching nipple with his palm.

"That feels good."

"That's only one way," he said, breaking to kiss her cheek, the tip of her nose. "I know more, but for you I want to invent things, brand-new ways to bring you to the brink. Over and over again."

He rolled farther onto his side, his still-hard erection startling against her thigh. His hand moved down her flank until he cupped her just above the back of her knee, and brought her leg up to rest on his hip. Then he slipped his hand between them, rubbing inside her with his thumb, then circling her swollen clit.

"You're everything I missed about this town," he said, thrusting slowly against her as she couldn't help responding to the insistent pressure exactly where she needed it. "I tried to forget I'd ever lived here, ever heard of Blackfoot Falls, but the memory of you kept pulling me back."

"We were so young," she said, her head lolling back as he nibbled a path down her neck.

"Too young," he whispered.

The pressure between her legs grew more intense, and she could already feel the heat pooling deep inside her. She realized she was squeezing the life out of his biceps, but she couldn't help it, not when she was gasping and arching and so, so close. "Oh, *God*," she said, the spasms stealing her thoughts and her air, but it was perfect. Perfect.

"Rachel," he whispered, as he lifted her knee and his thick heat slid inside her. The next quake had him moaning low and long.

When he was all the way in, she used her calf to bring him closer still. His open mouth came down between her neck and shoulder, and her body stifled his cry.

She was the one to move first. Not even a heartbeat went by before he took over. Once they'd established a pulsing rhythm, he raised his head, looked at her with his dark dilated eyes and his need, and kissed her until she could barely stand the pleasure.

It didn't take long. They'd been too keyed up for that, but she didn't give a damn. She could feel his body getting ready, hear it in his breathing as he released her mouth with a gasp. Even though the aftershocks were still coming in waves, she struggled to keep her eyes open, to see him abandoned and vulnerable. To watch as he came apart.

His head went back with a silent scream and his body stilled and trembled at the same time. If she hadn't climaxed already, she would have exploded just from this moment. To know this about him. To have the memory stored away.

She buried her face against his neck, and held him as tightly as she dared. There was no way to tell how long it was before his hand moved down her back, those rough hands so gentle it brought tears to her eyes.

For tonight she'd pretend Matt was hers. And she was his. Since it was make-believe, she threw in that it would be forever.

15

MATT DROPPED RACHEL OFF at the Sundance shortly after dawn. They knew by now almost everyone would have heard about what happened outside the Watering Hole so they weren't trying to be sneaky. Neither of them had slept much, but Rachel had wanted to get home before the guests woke and started asking questions.

On his way to the Lone Wolf, he found a bottle of aspirin in the glove compartment and downed three of the suckers. He'd refused to take anything in front of Rachel. She would've blamed herself and made a big deal out of every little twinge. He'd taken a mild beating last night, plain and simple. He'd seen red and fought angry. This was partly his fault. It didn't mean he wouldn't make Wallace fire those guys' asses.

Oh, Matt knew Wallace would argue, but maybe it was time for the old man to see another side of his son. Because those two were leaving even if Matt had to tie them to the bumper of his truck.

Approaching the house he saw the SUV parked in front. The Dodge pickup belonging to one of the guys sat near the bunkhouse. Part of him had wondered if Tony and Eddie might've sneaked off sometime last night. But then why should they? Probably figured Wallace would back them up.

Matt turned off the engine but stayed behind the wheel for a minute, stuffing the anger that had begun to resurface. Thinking about Rachel soft and warm beneath him last night helped calm him. Man, he hadn't wanted to let her go this morning. He'd have kept her in bed all day with him if he could've gotten away with it. The sex had been incredible, but it wasn't even about that for him. She made him feel like a new man.

She hadn't changed. Not in all the ways that counted. She was still generous and caring and honest. And the way she defended him…hell, no one took his side like Rachel. He loved his mother, but he hadn't been blind to her limitations. When he was younger he'd resented that she never stuck up for him.

And Nikki was great. She was a damn fine sister, especially considering they'd known each other only two years. But Rachel? She was one of a kind. He doubted a day had ever passed that she hadn't believed in him.

The door of the bunkhouse opened and a hand he didn't recognize strolled toward the stables. Matt waited until no one was in sight before he got out. He wanted to give Wallace the skinny on last night before he saw anyone else.

Inside was quiet, and he'd hoped to smell coffee brewing. He started a pot himself, then checked Wallace's office. He wasn't anywhere on the first floor, so Matt took the stairs—too fast, because his bruised ribs burned like a mother. Damn, he hoped confronting Wallace's guard dogs didn't get physical. If it came to that, Matt knew he could count on Petey, though he'd hate to put the guy in the middle.

Wallace's bedroom door was open. Matt ducked his head in to make sure he wasn't asleep or passed out, or hell, even dead. The last thought jarred Matt more than he would've guessed.

The bed was empty, unmade, and the adjoining bathroom door was open. Matt called out but got no answer. When Wallace wasn't hungover, he tended to be an early riser and drank coffee first thing. Matt crossed the room and confirmed the old man wasn't passed out on the bathroom floor.

He took the stairs slower this time, pausing for a look out the front windows. There was more activity outside, but he saw neither his father nor the two men, so he filled a mug and went back to Wallace's office. He'd show up sooner or later, and Matt figured once he'd finished his coffee, he'd stretch out on the couch with his eyes closed while he waited.

Taking a sip, he poked around the room, which was cleaner now, thanks to Lucy. Even the papers on the desk had been stacked in neat piles. Matt noticed a ledger and remembered Wallace hated computers and used spreadsheets instead. The financial condition of the Lone Wolf was none of Matt's business, but he wanted to know where things stood if Nikki were to eventually take over.

He moved around to the other side of the desk. The middle drawer was partially open, and his gaze caught on a newspaper clipping. It was a picture of Matt from an old *Houston Chronicle* column. He opened the drawer all the way and found a whole stack of articles from different newspapers, even copies of blogs. Sifting through them, he saw that they went back to the beginning of his career.

Shocked, he set down his mug. Wallace had never said a word to him. Not when Matt had returned to his mother's sickbed or after she'd passed. Of course Matt knew his father was aware of his success. No getting away from the talk in a place like Blackfoot Falls, but the man had said nothing. Not a word. Would it have killed him to have once told Matt he was proud of him?

A few of the clippings were worn with age, but they'd been preserved by plastic sleeves. He had to laugh when he saw that an earlier article had been torn in half and crumpled, then taped back together. Could've been his mother or Lucy who'd rescued the clipping. Though that didn't change the fact that Wallace had kept it.

The sudden and unwelcome lump in Matt's throat pissed him off. Too little, too late as far as he was concerned. If he hadn't been poking around he wouldn't even have known the old man gave a rat's ass about him. He stuffed the articles back into the drawer. He'd long passed the point of trying to please the stubborn bastard, damned if he was going to let this make him soft.

What was important now was dealing with the men from last night. Nikki wouldn't want to set foot on the place until they'd cleared out, and Matt didn't blame her. He thought he heard the kitchen door slam, and grabbed his mug.

Wallace stood at the sink washing his hands.

"We have to talk," Matt said, tensing, ready for an argument. For all he knew, Tony and Eddie had already given him their version of events.

Wearing Levi's and an untucked shirt, his hair uncombed, Wallace turned to him and snorted. "Good morning."

"Now." Matt walked past him to the coffeepot.

"Can I dry my hands first?"

He ignored the sarcastic tone, even figured he might've deserved it. He wasn't being smart. No sense heading in with a stick up his ass. "You want a cup?"

"Yeah, I'll take one."

Matt could feel his father pausing to eye him, then he heard the refrigerator door open. Wallace set a carton of cream on the counter and got a spoon out of the drawer.

"You used to drink coffee black," Matt said, and slid the steaming mug toward him.

"My gut can't take it anymore." Wallace frowned at him. "What happened to you?"

So he hadn't heard. Matt let out a breath. "There was an incident last night," he said, "outside the Watering Hole."

"You were fighting?"

Matt almost smiled at the surprised expression. Yeah, as if the old buzzard hadn't gotten into his share when he was younger. "It was one of your guys," Matt said, holding on to his anger when skepticism crossed Wallace's features.

"Who?"

"Eddie." Matt watched Wallace lean heavily against the counter and felt a moment's pity. But then he looked into the flagrant disbelief in his face and the sympathy vanished. "He was bothering Nikki. I stepped in."

Wallace seemed confused, his gaze wandering out the window. "What did he want with her?"

"I didn't stop to ask. When I drove up, she was trying to get away from him. Does he know she's your daughter?" Matt wasn't sure why he asked. It didn't matter.

"Nobody knows," Wallace murmured, still staring off. "Was Tony there?"

"He came out of the bar while Eddie and I were fighting."

"He jumped you?"

"To be fair, I don't think he knew Eddie had put his hands on Nikki." Matt gave a noncommittal shrug. "But the way I see it, he's gotta go, too."

Wallace met his gaze. "Is she okay?"

Matt nearly dropped his mug. He hadn't expected the question, or the concern in his father's eyes. "She grabbed a two-by-four and was ready to beat the shit out of 'em."

A faint smile tugged at Wallace's withered lips.

The pressure in Matt's chest eased. "You understand you have to fire them."

For a moment, Wallace looked torn, but then he nodded. His brief indecision was enough to get Matt's temper sparked. But he talked himself down, remembering that his father had come to depend on the two men. The bastard had never needed anyone before, and God knew he deserved to be humbled, but Matt wouldn't gloat.

"Well, let's go, son." Wallace set down the coffee he'd barely touched. "I suspect it'll give you some satisfaction to do the deed yourself."

Shocked, Matt stared. Had he heard right? Son? What the hell was that about? He shoved his questions aside to concentrate on what he was about to do and prepared for trouble.

He followed Wallace out the kitchen door to the bunkhouse. Wallace had one of the wranglers call Eddie and Tony to come outside. The men had been asleep, and Matt was pleased to see the swelling in Eddie's jaw, the bruising around his right eye. That he looked hungover, too, was icing on the cake.

"You have an hour to pack and get off the Lone Wolf," he said without preamble. "Go quietly and no charges will be filed."

The men were stupid enough to look shocked.

His bloodshot eyes brimming with malice, Eddie glowered at Wallace. "You don't wanna do this, old man."

His father had never backed down in his life. But Wallace actually seemed a little cowed. His jaw set, he shook his head. "You shouldn't have touched her," he said to Eddie, then looked to Tony. "Nikki's my daughter."

Tony cursed, and shot a disgusted look at his friend, who hadn't stopped glaring. It made the hair on the back of Matt's neck stand up. The guy didn't scare him, but Matt had the strange feeling something else was going on he didn't understand and that bothered him.

"I'll have your final checks ready." Wallace spoke only to Tony, who nodded, his expression resigned.

"Come on, Eddie." He bumped his friend's shoulder.

Matt touched his dad's arm, and they both turned to walk back to the house. Nothing left to do but hope Eddie didn't cause trouble and be prepared if he did. "Thanks," Matt murmured. "For doing right by Nikki."

"You think you can get her to come back here?" Wallace asked, his head down, his feet shuffling. "I'd like to talk to her."

"I can try." Matt watched Wallace take an unsteady step onto the flagstone walkway leading to the porch, and dammit, another pang of pity undercut him. Not that he was softening. The years of hate and resentment ran too deep. But Wallace had asked to see Nikki. Matt was glad to see him making an effort, that's all. "Can you stay sober till then?"

He sighed as if the whole world had been dumped on his shoulders. "I can try."

FROM THE SECOND FLOOR, Rachel saw Matt's truck coming down the drive and she raced downstairs. At his second knock she opened the door and almost threw her arms around him before she remembered his ribs.

His one eye seemed more bruised but the swelling had subsided. The stubble on his jaw hid the scrapes he'd suffered from his face being jammed into the sidewalk. He still looked great to her and she wanted to kiss him. Very badly.

"You gonna make me stand out here?" he asked, his mouth twisting in a lopsided smile as he pulled the hat off his head.

"Oh." She laughed and stepped back. "You look pretty good, considering. Did you get some sleep? Have you been icing?"

"Yes on both counts." He stopped in front of her, took a quick look around, then tipped her chin up and kissed her lips.

It was too brief, though they were standing in the middle of the foyer, and she couldn't help glancing over her shoulder.

"No one saw."

"I don't know why I did that. I am legal age, after all."

"You sure? You still look like jailbait to me."

"Huh, after only four hours of sleep…" Scoffing, Rachel touched the outside corner of her right eye. "I have laugh lines and I'm probably as puffy as you are."

Matt chuckled. "Gee, thanks."

"You're laughing without wincing. That's great." She ran her gaze over his chest, liking his blue Western-cut shirt. He wore new jeans, too. "How are your ribs?"

"Good, better than I thought they'd be." His smoldering look gave her a shiver that involved every part of her body. Either he was thinking about last night or what he intended to do to her now that he was feeling better. "You're blushing."

"Am I?" She cleared her throat and moved toward the living room. "Why are you dressed up?"

He'd followed her, as she expected, but she wasn't prepared for him to cup the back of her neck. He pulled her into a kiss, and she automatically clung to his shoulders, barely able to breathe until he was finished with her.

"Happy Valentine's Day," he whispered, brushing the stray curls off her warm cheeks, his gaze locked on her face.

"Giving me a heart attack on Valentine's Day hardly seems appropriate."

"I promise you that's not what I had in mind." With a smile, he moved his hand, and casually fingered the rim of his Stetson. Her thoughts flashed to last night. He had very clever hands, and she had to order herself to stop. No thinking. Not about yesterday or last night. God help her. "What time's the dance?"

"Seven." She checked out his fancy duds again. "You know it's only three-thirty, right?"

"I have to talk to Nikki for a few minutes and then I was hoping you'd go for a drive with me. Maybe have dinner in Kalispell, then go to the dance afterward."

She groaned. "Kalispell won't work. I can't get ready in time."

"I understand. It's last-minute." He smiled. "Can we go for a drive before the dance?"

She nodded, excited. "Sure. Want me to get Nikki?"

"I'm here. I got your voice mail."

Rachel turned and saw his sister coming down the stairs.

She'd taken a nap after helping Hilda make lunch. "I know Cole won't mind if you want to use his office," Rachel said, assuming they needed privacy.

"The den is fine." Matt's gaze stayed on Nikki.

Rachel stepped back. "I'll leave you—"

"This won't take long," Nikki said, her blank expression somehow communicating something to Matt, because he sighed as if he'd just gotten an answer he didn't want. "You can stay."

"I probably shouldn't," Rachel murmured, moving back. Yes, she was nosy as hell but she wouldn't intrude.

"We fired them," Matt said before Rachel could escape. "Eddie and Tony are both gone. And Wallace asked to see you."

"We?" Nikki frowned. "He made you do it? He didn't have the guts to—"

"It wasn't like that. He figured it would give me some satisfaction." He shrugged, a hint of a smile tugging at his mouth. "Wallace didn't argue. He was pissed that Eddie had touched you."

Rachel stared at him. He seemed really relaxed. She doubted it had to do with firing the men, but rather he was pleased with Wallace's response. It wasn't so much his words but his tone of voice that made her take notice. So had Nikki, it seemed.

Her chin lifted. "If I go over there, will he be drunk?"

"Said he'd try and stay sober." Matt concentrated on pressing the rim of his Stetson with his thumb and forefinger, then looked up. "Give him another chance. Can't hurt."

Nikki breathed in deeply. "Well, he did fire those guys." She sighed. "I haven't thanked him for the money. I suppose I should do that at least. Doesn't mean I've forgiven him, though."

At the mention of money, Rachel noticed Matt stiffen. But he maintained a neutral expression, and she doubted Nikki had caught the slight shift. She was too busy sorting her own emotions.

"I told him you were probably busy with the dance tonight, and he seemed whipped himself. Lucy is over there now," Matt said, clearly distracted. "Maybe tomorrow morning…"

"Yeah, that's better than today. I need to psych myself up." Nikki pushed her hair back. "Rachel, I do want to help. It keeps my mind off stuff. If you want to go with Matt—"

"It's not that." Rachel glanced regretfully at him. "I wanted a little time to get ready."

"Ah, girl stuff." Matt smiled, and threaded a lingering hand through her hair. "You look damn good to me already."

She rolled her eyes. "Give me an hour. I'll call."

"I'll be waiting." He kissed her again, this time lightly brushing her lips. "Can I do anything?"

"Yes, get out of here." Rachel hadn't realized she'd put her hands on his chest. She gave him a small shove toward the front door. "You're distracting me."

Nikki had already headed for the kitchen, but not before Rachel caught her grin.

"All right." He settled his hat on his head. "I'm going." But he didn't move. "One more kiss first?"

"No." Rachel walked him backward through the foyer. "Okay, one," she said, grabbing the front of his shirt and pulling him down for a quick peck. What a fool. Of course now she wanted more. She opened the door. "Goodbye."

He just laughed, walked onto the porch and turned to give her a wink before she closed the door.

She'd been silly enough over him before they'd made love. Now, Lord have mercy… Even if she'd tried to keep their relationship low-key, she doubted she could hide a thing. She actually felt giddy around him, like she had at sixteen. Tonight would be interesting. Half the people in town had probably heard about the fight. She wondered just how many knew they'd spent the night at Noah's.

Sighing, she took a peek out the window at his retreating back, then spun around and met her mother's concerned gaze.

"Oh." Rachel put a hand to her chest. "You startled me."

"I'm sorry, honey. I just came from the kitchen."

Rachel wondered how much she'd seen, though it didn't matter…except why the worried frown? "Did you need me?"

"Actually, Jamie was looking for you." She glanced toward the window. "I'm sorry I missed Matt."

"You'll see him at the dance tonight." Rachel moved closer to her mom. "I meant to ask…that day he spoke to you privately—"

Jamie came bounding down the stairs. "Glad I caught you. We need to talk," she said, then did a double take on Barbara to her left. "Sorry, I didn't see you. Am I interrupting?"

"No," her mom said quickly, then to Rachel, "I'm not comfortable discussing the conversation."

"I understand." Rachel blushed. "I shouldn't have asked."

Jamie turned and started back up the stairs.

"Wait," Rachel said, at the same time her mom said, "You girls talk. I have an errand to run in town."

Rachel and Jamie watched Barbara leave before Jamie said, "I have to book Tahiti by Monday at the latest so I need to know what you want to do. The trip's only three weeks away."

"Tahiti?" Rachel frowned, having trouble shifting gears.

"We talked about it, remember?" Jamie's voice lowered. "About you taking the trip while I cover for you here."

Rachel had completely forgotten. Four days ago the idea had sounded fabulous. But that was before Matt showed up. And, God help her, now she couldn't think of anything or anyone else.

16

MATT TURNED THE TRUCK into the gravel driveway of the ranch he'd found on an online real estate site. He hadn't told Rachel yet why they were here, and he'd misjudged how much time it would take to cross the county line. Damn his impulsiveness. They'd have to turn around in five minutes to make it back to the dance.

It was nice having her sit close, being able to touch her when he wanted, steal a kiss when he could take his eyes off the road. A couple times, even when he shouldn't have.

"Where are we?" She twisted around to look out the back window. "I saw a For Sale sign back there."

"Yep, it's been on the market for over a year. Only twelve hundred acres, but that's decent."

She remained quiet for so long, he looked over at her. She stared back, her expression confused but also worried. "Are you looking for yourself?"

Matt shrugged. "I mentioned I want to raise rodeo stock at some point. I always figured it would be in Texas, but I'm weighing my options."

They drove in silence until a barn came into view. There were several other buildings to the right, but he wasn't half as interested in them as he was in the reason for her silence. He'd expected more enthusiasm.

"Are you meeting with a Realtor?" she asked finally.

"No, we don't have time. I just wanted a look-see before I made an appointment." He glanced at her tense profile. "*If* I make one. I haven't really decided." Did she feel that he'd wasted her time? "Sorry I brought you out this far."

"Don't be silly." She laid a hand on his thigh and smiled at him. "I enjoyed the ride."

He was disappointed, no getting around it. He didn't know what she was thinking, and he didn't want to ask. What bothered him most was that he couldn't figure out what was going through her mind. He'd been better at it ten years ago.

This was not turning out to be his day. First, Nikki mentioned the money both he and his mother had secretly sent, about which he'd neglected to set her straight. And now Rachel wasn't reacting at all like he'd pictured. Did she think this sudden change of heart was about her? That he might be trying to pin her down?

Hell, even if some part of him wanted to return to Montana on account of her, he knew better. Not only did she have too much going for her, she'd made it pretty clear the first night what she thought about guys from Blackfoot Falls. He couldn't be mad, though. He'd always known he wasn't good enough for her.

He found a place to turn around and swerved the truck into the small clearing.

"What are you doing? Don't you want a closer look?"

Matt finished the U-turn. "I found it online this morning while I was screwing around. No big deal."

"It's me, right? I ruined it by not being more excited."

"What?" he drawled. "Come here." He slid an arm around her shoulders, drew her close and kissed her hair. "You didn't ruin anything."

"I was just surprised, is all. I swear."

He believed her. He also knew there was more to her reaction, but he didn't have it in him to ask. "This morning, when I was looking for my father, I found a stack of clippings in his office. The son of a bitch has been following my career all along and never said a word to me."

Rachel lifted her head off his shoulder and looked at him. "Did you say anything?"

"Nah, what's the point? I was just glad he didn't give me grief over firing those two idiots. I could tell he didn't want to do it, and I know why from Lucy, but he manned up, so I give him credit for that. He actually called me 'son'—did I tell you?" He glanced at her when she didn't respond.

She had that worried frown again. But then she smiled and it was gone. "What did Lucy say?"

"Wallace can't drive anymore, or at least shouldn't be driving. Eddie and Tony took him everywhere, even to doctor's appointments. She asked if I planned on sticking around and taking up the slack." He knew Rachel was watching him, waiting for him to elaborate. But it was her reaction that interested him.

"Can't Lucy drive him to his appointments?" she asked.

"Yeah, but she's not going to take him to barhop in Kalispell."

"Would you?"

"No," he said, sharply. "I can stick around awhile, and only because he's been acting decent. But I have to ride in Houston in a couple of weeks. Then there's Nikki to consider. They're gonna talk tomorrow, and I hope my dad doesn't screw it up. No telling which way that'll go."

Something was bothering Rachel. Silence stretched between them, and he wished she'd put it out there already. He was about to ask when she said, "Is he well enough to be carousing?"

"I don't know. I haven't asked him about his prognosis. Figured I'd see how it went with Nikki first." Matt applied pressure to the knot tightening the side of his neck.

Man, he hoped she didn't bring up the money to Wallace. Odds were he'd piss her off in the first few minutes and that would be that. Matt would hate to see their meeting play out that way, even if it did let him off the hook. He probably should just get it over with and confess to Nikki. She'd be mad...that was a given, but if her bad mood carried over into tomorrow that would be on Matt.

It occurred to him to ask for Rachel's thoughts on what he should do. At least it would break the damn quiet. "I need your advice. I might've done a bonehead thing," he said, glancing over to see her lips curve in a smile. "Okay, no snide remarks."

"Nope. Go ahead."

"My mom secretly sent money to Nikki's mother to help out. After she passed, I never saw a reason to tell Nikki that I took over and now she thinks it was Wallace sending the money orders. If she says something to him, I'm gonna be in hot water."

"Yes, I imagine you will."

He sighed. "She thinks he was decent enough to send child support. If I tell her the truth, she might not want to see him."

Rachel looked away, drawing in a deep breath. "She's a grown woman. She can handle the truth." She turned back to him, her expression troubled again. "In fact, she deserves the truth, Matt."

"But why hurt her if I don't have to, especially if there's a chance it won't even come up?"

"It sounds as if you've made up your mind," she said, a trace of sadness in her voice. Did she think he was a coward?

"Not true." He sighed. "You're right. I'll tell her. Not tonight, though. Let her enjoy the dance. And me, too. I don't need my ass kicked two nights in a row."

That made her smile again. She slid closer, picked up his

arm and adjusted it around her shoulders. "Did I mention you have a very cute ass?"

Matt laughed, squeezing her closer and soaking up her warmth, her mysterious feminine scent. Being with Rachel always made everything better. Always.

THEY ARRIVED AT THE DANCE on time. Rachel had planned on being there early to help the Lemon sisters, prepare the punch, make coffee and set out heart-shaped sugar cookies and chocolate cupcakes with pink icing. But Jamie and Nikki were there pitching in.

The place looked nice with white tablecloths to hide the old folding tables, clusters of red balloons tied around posts and the red and pink foil hearts floating down from the beams. She expected to get a few complaints about the strobe lighting confined to one corner of the dance floor, but she'd convinced the other "committee members" to let some of the high school kids be involved this year. Even the band was made up of four senior boys.

More people than expected had turned out. Maybe it was the unseasonably warm weather, or the influx of available young women from the Sundance that brought in more cowhands than past years.

But Rachel suspected quite a few folks had come because they wanted to see Matt. He was a local hero, whether he liked it or not. He didn't seem comfortable in the role, unless it was kids asking him questions about the rodeo circuit. And when one of the high school boys called him a rodeo rock star, poor Matt had actually blushed.

Grinning, Rachel stepped in to save him, "Hey, cowboy, how about a dance?"

He didn't seem thrilled. "I must be getting old. What kind of music is that?"

She hadn't really been listening and saw that the dance floor had thinned out. The band seemed to be having a good time, rocking out as if they were the only ones in the room. "Those boys…darn it…I told them no hip-hop. I'll be right back."

By the time she got the music back on track, Matt was surrounded by another group of admirers, two kids and a pair of guests from the Sundance. Rachel didn't rush to his aid this time. First she scolded a couple of pranksters who were filching the red foil hearts and popping balloons, then she stood back, idly watching him while she thought about their ride earlier.

She was so worried for him it made her ache. After all that had happened, after all this time, he still yearned for his father's approval. Oh, he'd deny it if she were to point it out. But it wasn't her imagination that he'd lit up when talking about the newspaper clippings Wallace had saved, or how he'd called Matt "son." She wondered if Matt realized that he'd referred to Wallace as Dad. It sure had surprised her.

The whole thing made her uneasy because she didn't want to see Matt set himself up for another fall. And yes, she hated that he was willing to accept crumbs from the selfish bastard. The mere idea made her angry and so sad she didn't know what to do with all the conflicting emotions.

And the thing with Nikki? Rachel had no doubt Matt loved his sister. Yet he was ready to test their relationship by hiding the truth about Wallace's callous abandonment of his daughter. It wasn't just about keeping the peace so they could talk or protecting Nikki. Matt was protecting Wallace, too. Protecting the fragile new bond Matt had always craved.

If it gave him the closure he needed, she supposed it wasn't horrible for him to believe Wallace had changed. Perhaps faced with mortality the man had evolved to some degree. But something else concerned her. Yesterday he'd been resigned to the short time Wallace had left. Today Matt was looking to buy a nearby ranch.

She honestly didn't know what to make of that. Or why he

hadn't even mentioned the Lone Wolf. All she knew for sure was that her reaction had disappointed him. She'd been too stunned to even fake enthusiasm. But she'd fix it later. The last thing she wanted was for him to feel he couldn't confide in her.

"I thought we were going to dance."

She blinked, startled that she hadn't seen Matt come up to her. "We are, but I'd prefer something a bit slower."

"Yeah, me too." He glanced around at the couples sitting at the tables. Several older teenagers hovered suspiciously close to the punch bowl. "Weird how many people I don't know." His gaze briefly rested on two cowboys talking to Lisa, a blonde from Albuquerque, who gave him a small wave. "I'm not just talking about your guests."

"Even I had trouble when I moved back. And I made it home every summer and holidays. Nikki seems to be having a good time."

Matt followed Rachel's gaze to the back corner and smiled when he saw his sister talking to three guys. Nikki wore a snug red dress that she'd borrowed from Jamie, and Rachel wished she herself had made the effort to wear something nicer than new jeans and a blue sweater. Trouble was, it was still winter and she didn't own an appropriate dress. She had quite a few short strappy numbers from Dallas, bought when her plans had included a career someplace warmer and more exotic.

She thought about Tahiti, and Jamie's terrific offer, and sighed. Why did the timing have to stink? Fat chance she'd get an opportunity like it again, but she couldn't see herself having a good time thousands of miles away knowing Matt was here.

"What was that for?" He touched her cheek.

"Oh, were my eyes glazed over?" She laughed at herself. "I feel badly about earlier…when you showed me the ranch. I should've been more enthusiastic and not so selfish." She smiled at his confused frown. "You're making life awfully difficult for me. If you move back, how am I supposed to leave?"

He studied her face for what seemed like an hour before he turned his gaze toward the crowded dance floor.

Panic fisted in her chest. He'd kept his expression carefully neutral but she had the horrible feeling she knew what had spooked him. "You know I'm teasing, right? This thing between us—" She shrugged a shoulder. "I know it's not serious, so you don't have to rush home and pack or anything."

Matt turned back to her with a smile. "You still want to dance, or go make out in the back of the hardware store?"

She laughed, the pressure in her chest easing. "No making out until later. And only if you're good."

He leaned into her. "I thought I proved that yesterday."

The look on his face made her heart flutter, and she glanced around to see who might be watching. It was stupid because at this point almost everyone in town probably knew they'd spent the night together at Noah's.

"Relax," he whispered. "I won't embarrass you."

She huffed. "Why would you say that? Half the women here are envious as hell and would love to lock me in a closet so they can have you." She wasn't lying, despite his patronizing smirk.

"I don't believe it." Matt motioned with his chin.

She turned and saw that Jamie had gotten Cole on the dance floor, which was a shock. As usual, Trace was surrounded by his admirers, both local women and Sundance guests.

"Who's that?" Matt asked, peering toward the door. "She's not a local but she doesn't look like a Sundance guest either."

"Oh, that's Annie Sheridan. I want you to meet her." Rachel waved until she got the blonde's attention. "She runs Safe Haven. It's a large animal sanctuary east of Cy Heber's ranch. Was the place there before you left?"

"Yeah, but somebody else ran it, a man from Boise, I think."

"Annie's been there about two years now. She's done an amazing job. I don't know where she's from. She's very private, hardly ever comes to town unless she needs something for the animals. Hey, you." Rachel stepped back to include Annie. "I can't believe you came."

"I figured I'd pop in for a bit. I'm a sucker for chocolate cupcakes." Annie's gaze went directly to Matt. "Hi." Rachel made the introductions, surprised at Annie's overt interest in Matt. Then she got it and had to hide a smile. Annie was going to hit Matt up for something, and Rachel didn't blame her.

"I've heard a lot about you from the Safe Haven volunteers," Annie said. "Will you be sticking around awhile?"

It was kind of adorable how Matt moved a little closer to Rachel, either for protection or to let Annie know he was taken. "Not sure yet," he said. "I understand you're doing quite a job out there."

"I'm trying," she said, letting out a sigh and sweeping the pale hair away from her tanned face. "We have limited funds, and sometimes I have to refuse or relocate animals. It kills me, but I do my best."

Matt nodded, gave her worn jeans, gray sweatshirt and work boots a discreet once-over. That her clothes were clean was her nod to a social occasion. "Thank God for people like you. I don't have my checkbook on me but I'll make a donation later."

"Thanks. We need all the help we can get." She was so pretty, wore almost no makeup, and even with her long gorgeous hair pulled into a ponytail, she looked as if she should be doing shampoo commercials instead of pitching hay.

Rachel wasn't the only one who wondered how Annie had landed in Blackfoot Falls, or where she'd come from, other than "back east." But Annie kept her mouth shut and never invited personal questions.

They chatted a few more minutes, mostly small talk while they watched the dancers. Several people stopped to say they were glad to see Annie doing something other than work. A few guys tried to get her on the floor. She refused them all and then started looking itchy to leave.

"Matt, I have a question for you," Annie said. "Do you know anything about the benefit rodeos they have down South?"

He nodded. "I'm riding in one in two weeks."

"How does a charity get in on that? Is it one rodeo, one charity, or are profits split?"

Smiling, Rachel listened to them talk. She'd bet Annie knew everything there was to know about the subject, but this was why she was so damn good at raising money for the sanctuary. They finished, then Annie said her goodbyes. She left without a cupcake, but with Matt's promise that he'd put something together for her locally this summer.

To Rachel that meant he'd be back, and already she was getting giddy and jittery inside knowing she'd see him.

He shook his head and started laughing as he stared after Annie. "That woman had me volunteering before I knew what I was doing. She's good."

"Yes, she is. Maybe I should've warned you."

"I don't mind helping out." He turned his attention to Rachel. "Think you'll still be here this summer?"

"Oh, yeah, and probably the summer after that." She shrugged when sympathy entered his eyes. "It's really not been bad."

"Talk Cole into raising rodeo stock. It's good money, and you can shut down the dude ranch."

"Trying to get rid of me?"

"Never." He lifted a hand and barely touched her hair before abruptly pulling back. "There's something I wanted to ask Annie. Maybe we can still catch her. Come with me."

"I have her phone number," she said, but he tugged at her hand and wouldn't let go until they were outside.

The big round moon cast the clear sky in a soft romantic glow. It was a little chilly but still a perfect Valentine's night. Even more perfect because Matt was here. Once they were away from the door, he took her hand again and led her around the parked cars and trucks to get to the side of the barn. They saw only two men leaning against a pickup smoking and swapping stories across the road. Where Matt took her was dim and private.

Rachel smiled. "I don't think we'll find Annie back here."

"I lied." He pulled her close and kissed her mouth, slowly, teasing her with the tip of his tongue. "You're the one I want."

"And whatever will you do with me?"

"I tell you and you'll be blushing until next Sunday."

Laughing, she pressed against him, thrilled that he was already hard. "Glad we're thinking along the same lines."

"How long do we have to hang around?" He trailed his damp lips down the side of her neck, his lightly bearded jaw grazing her skin. He'd apologized for not shaving because of the scrapes. But if he knew how hot he looked he'd never touch a razor again.

She sighed with pleasure, then stiffened when she heard voices nearby. Sounded like Nikki's and a man. Matt obviously heard them, too. He lifted his head just as Nikki said, "Get away from me."

"STAY HERE," MATT SAID, holding on to Rachel's upper arms; his gaze was level with hers. "Please."

She didn't answer, and he figured she'd end up following him, but he couldn't waste time arguing.

He found his sister just around the corner of the barn, not far from the door where a light shone. Tony, one of the men he'd fired this morning, stood in front of her.

"Look," he said to Nikki, holding both hands up, palms out. "I just wanted to apologize. I had no idea Eddie had messed with you. If I had, I would've kicked his ass myself."

"Fine. You said it." Nikki's arms were folded, her chin lifted. "So leave."

"Don't worry. He is." Matt stopped a few feet away.

Nikki shot him a startled look. "Oh, God, Matt. Come on, don't." She got in between them. "Tony wanted to apologize. That's all."

"Yeah, well, Tony shouldn't even be here," Matt said. "The deal was that you and Eddie get out of town immediately."

Tony glared at him. "You didn't have to fire us, Gunderson. Eddie was drunk, no excuse, but we could've worked it out."

The door opened, and Trace walked outside.

Nikki groaned. "Oh, great."

"Nothing's gonna happen," Matt said, and he wasn't lying. Tony looked pissed, but Matt could tell the guy wasn't looking for a fight. "Trace, take Nikki inside. Tony's just leaving." Matt glanced over his shoulder. Sure enough, Rachel had followed right behind him.

Nikki marched past Trace to go back to the dance, ignoring something he said to her. Trace moved backward but he didn't go inside.

"Tell you what, Gunderson," Tony said, stepping in close so that only Matt could hear. "You oughtta get off your high horse and figure out what's really going on at the Lone Wolf."

17

MATT WOKE LATER THAN usual the next morning feeling as if he hadn't slept. Between thinking about Rachel and stewing over what Tony had said, he'd managed to grab about four hours.

The dance hadn't lasted past eleven but everything had started going wrong at around nine. Two seniors from the high school ended up spiking the punch and the band kept trying to sneak in rap songs.

None of it was tragic, but Rachel had been dragged into the middle of every lousy squabble, meaning he'd spent too little time with her. Then he hadn't even driven her home, which pissed him off the most. Her mother, Cole and Jamie had helped with cleanup and then Barbara had Rachel in her car before Matt knew what had happened.

He had a strong suspicion the exit had been planned. Maybe on account of him and Rachel staying at Noah's the night before and Barbara worrying about what people would think. Though he'd been careful not to stand too close or allow any lingering touches. And Rachel had been on guard, as well. For the most part, they hadn't broadcast anything. So maybe he was just being paranoid. Everyone had been tired, including him. Even Nikki had ducked out early.

The aroma of coffee wafted up to his room, and he pulled

on jeans and a flannel shirt, then went downstairs. No one was in the kitchen. But there was a full pot of fresh brew and a note from Lucy that she'd taken Wallace to the doctor in Kalispell.

Matt felt a moment's guilt. That was something he should've done, but then Wallace hadn't mentioned the appointment. Taking a steaming mug with him to the front windows, he surveyed the barn, corrals and stables. In the distance a handful of men were fixing some equipment near the calving shed, and Matt idly wondered how many heifers were expected to drop calves this spring.

Inevitably his thoughts went back to Tony's warning last night. Matt was tempted to talk to Petey about it, but if Petey knew of anything hinky going on he would've said.

He put on his boots, refilled his mug, pulled on his jacket and headed toward the barn. He stopped to talk with a couple of the hands who were fueling the four-wheelers while he glanced around. In the stables a kid mucking the stalls barely spared him a look. Petey was nowhere in sight—another wrangler thought he might've ridden to the north pasture an hour ago.

So Matt continued to poke around, checking out the state of the ranch's equipment. Everything seemed well maintained. The animals all looked healthy. The welfare of their animals had always been a sore spot for him since some folks had accused his father of mistreatment. He personally had never witnessed Wallace abuse or neglect an animal.

By the time Matt walked over to a large isolated storage shed past the main buildings, he was pretty sure Tony had gotten the last laugh. The Lone Wolf seemed in good shape and was being manned by competent hands. Since he was there anyway, he decided to look inside. But the door was padlocked. Twice.

He didn't remember the shed being here before, but that meant nothing. It probably housed new equipment. But why the double lock? There were large tire tracks in the hardened mud from before the recent snowfall. He wouldn't rest easy until he knew what was inside so he jogged toward the house, swinging by the barn first.

The men inside pitching hay thought the shed hadn't been used since last summer, so he went on to Wallace's office. A ring of keys hung from a nail behind the door and he figured one of them might open the padlocks.

This time he took the long route to the shed, hoping he could get a look inside without anyone seeing him. No one seemed to pay him any mind. After trying three keys, he found the ones that popped the padlocks.

He opened the door just enough to slip inside and then pulled the string to a bare lightbulb. In the middle of the shed was a big horse trailer, flanked by a small flatbed with good saddles carelessly tossed on top and a late model four-wheeler. Tack had been scattered on the floor that should've been hanging in the stables. Even the horse trailer belonged with the rest....

Matt stepped over a lead for a better look at the trailer. His heart nearly stopped. The trailer was the stolen Exiss that belonged to the McAllisters.

RACHEL HAD BEEN ANXIOUSLY watching for Matt's truck for ten minutes when she saw the telltale dust over the driveway. He'd sounded funny when he called to ask her to go for a ride, but he wouldn't say what was wrong.

She grabbed her jacket and went outside. He pulled the truck close to the porch, and she hopped in. Without a word he headed back down the driveway.

"Okay, you're officially scaring me." She barely had time to buckle her seat belt. "What's going on?"

Giving her a strained smile, he reached over and squeezed her hand. "I missed you. I wanted to drive you home last night."

"I know. That played out kind of weird." Staring at the muscle working in his jaw, she bit her lip. Her insides twisted so tight she had trouble breathing. "You're leaving, aren't you?"

He shot her a confused look. "Today? No." He brought her shaky hand to his lips. "No, Rachel. Not unless I get chased out of town," he said grimly. Then startled her by pulling the truck off the road.

They were still on Sundance property but it wasn't the wisest place to park. It was a straight road, though, so traffic coming either way was easy to spot. "Why are we stopping?"

Matt shifted closer, gathered her in his arms and buried his face in her hair. "I want to sink inside you so deep no one can pull us apart."

Her breath caught. "Um…wow." She really and truly didn't know what to say. But he took care of that by pressing his mouth to hers, as if this would be their last kiss.

She parted her lips for him, and he slipped his tongue inside, hot and demanding, as he swept over her teeth, swept everywhere, taking complete possession of her mouth. A parade could've passed and she wouldn't have noticed.

When he finally pulled back, he let out a harsh breath. "Sometimes life really sucks."

Still dazed from the magic of his kiss, she couldn't seem to make sense of what he'd just said. "Matt, tell me what's going on."

He rubbed his scraped jaw, tried to hide the devastation in his eyes. With a gentle touch, she guided his gaze back to hers.

"I'm gonna tell you something you won't want to hear, and you could hate me for…" He started to look away, but forced himself to stay with her. "And I'm going to be ballsy enough to ask you to keep it between us."

"Yes." She could never hate him. "Just tell me."

"Your horse trailer is sitting in a shed at the Lone Wolf."

"Which trailer?" She shook her head, then gasped. "The one that was stolen? The Exiss?"

Matt said nothing, just stared at her.

"How?" She didn't understand. "Why?"

"I don't know. Something Tony said last night bothered me so I looked around this morning…. There are other things… saddles and a flatbed, some expensive tack. I'm guessing they've all been stolen."

"What did your father say about it?"

"I haven't talked to him yet." He laid his head back on the headrest. "Lucy took him to a doctor's appointment in Kalispell."

"This doesn't make sense. What exactly did Tony tell you?"

"That I should get off my high horse and figure out what's really going on at the Lone Wolf."

"Well, obviously he had something to do with it, and Eddie, I'd imagine. But you kicked them out before they had a chance to sell off the…" Rachel sighed, her temples throbbing. "No, the thefts started last August and stopped right before Christmas. They've had plenty of time to get rid of everything. But why would he steer you toward evidence that would incriminate him?"

"He wouldn't…unless Wallace knows," he said bleakly.

"But he doesn't need any of the— Oh, God." An unpleasant thought hit her. "Noah and Cole suspected Avery Phelps of having something to do with the thefts because he wanted to get back at us for taking in guests. Right after we opened, our trailer went missing, and then other ranches started getting robbed."

"I'm not following," Matt said, frowning. "Although that's about the time Tony and Eddie hired on."

"Wallace and Avery never liked each other, but they started getting chummy, drinking at the Watering Hole together." She took a shaky breath, becoming more convinced Wallace was involved. "Avery couldn't have acted alone but he may have given your father the idea. A lot of folks started blaming us for bringing in crime along with the tourists."

Matt rubbed his eyes, his mouth set in a grim line.

"I'm just thinking out loud. Don't listen to me."

"It's okay, Rachel. I think we both know Wallace somehow had a hand in this."

"Look, my brothers and everyone else will just be so happy to get their property back. After that, who knows." She hated to point out the obvious. "I mean considering the circumstances."

Matt met her eyes. "I don't want anyone to know yet."

"What do you mean by yet?"

"I need time to talk to Wallace, and if necessary, sort things out with Noah when he gets back. I don't want Nikki to get caught in all this. She needs her chance to find closure."

She felt queasy recalling that he wanted the conversation kept between them. "We should tell Cole. He'll be angry but after we explain about your dad's health—"

He swore under his breath. "I shouldn't have told you."

"Of course you should have."

"But now I've put you in the middle." Matt stared out the windshield, shaking his head. "I'm such a selfish prick. Guess the apple really doesn't fall far from the tree."

"Don't you dare spout that crap." Now she was pissed. "I mean it. You know better."

He turned to her with a sad smile. "Give me twenty-four hours," he said, reaching for her hand. "I know what I'm asking, and it kills me to do it."

And it was killing her to agree. She nodded, feeling like the worst kind of traitor to her family. But this was Matt. And he could throw Nikki's name around all he wanted, but Rachel knew he needed the closure, too. Needed to feel he'd mattered to his father and that their tiny new bond was real.

She knew she was right, but that didn't lessen her guilt and it sure wouldn't help her sleep tonight. The McAllisters had always placed family first. Always. Everything had just gotten too damned complicated. Maybe she should think seriously about heading to Tahiti before she was banished from the Sundance.

"I THOUGHT YOU'D LEFT," Wallace said the next morning when he entered the kitchen, his shoulders stooped and his complexion pasty. Though he actually looked better than yesterday. The trip to Kalispell and two doctor's appointments had worn him out.

"In a few minutes." Matt sipped the coffee he'd just made. This was it…he had to lay his cards on the table. Maybe then he could quit stewing over the predicament he'd put Rachel in.

Maybe even get a good night's sleep himself. The upside was he'd been able to do a lot of thinking while he stared into the darkness as the hours ticked by. His dad hadn't been getting around much. It wasn't unreasonable to believe he was ignorant of the thefts or what Tony and Eddie had been up to.

"Seems as if you've got something on your mind, son." With a disinterested frown, Wallace looked up from the note and plate of bran muffins Lucy had left him. "You got something to say?"

"You heard about the thefts around the county, I'm sure."

Wallace concentrated on pouring his coffee, the tremor in his hand causing the liquid to slosh over the rim. "Yep."

"I have some bad news." Matt paused, waiting for a reaction he didn't get. "I found the stolen items here on the Lone Wolf."

His father had trouble setting down the coffeepot. "Where?"

"A locked shed in the back. You know anything about it?"

"No." His frail body shuddered and he gripped the edge of the counter. "Why would I need to steal? I run the only profitable ranch in this county. And by myself."

"I'm not accusing you of stealing," Matt said, trying to reconcile the man before him with the one who'd scared the shit out of him when he was a kid. Damn, he'd never thought he'd see the day Wallace would look so broken. Some of the fight left Matt and he knew he couldn't corner the guy and kick him while he was down. "I think your two boys, Tony and Eddie, might've been pulling one over on you."

Remaining silent, Wallace moved to the refrigerator for his milk.

"No need for you to worry about it," Matt said. "I just thought you should know. I'll make sure the property is returned to the victims. If everything is there, I doubt the sheriff will see fit to track anyone down. Those guys have to be long gone by now."

Wallace nodded, but kept his gaze averted. No way to tell if he was feeling guilty, or angry with himself for not seeing what had been going on under his own nose. And maybe Matt was nothing but a damn fool. But he hadn't wanted a blowup. The guy was dying. What did any of it matter? All Matt wanted was to clear things up with Rachel and let his sister make peace with the old man.

"I'll go get Nikki." Matt drained his mug and stood, then heard an engine. He went to the window. "She's here. Must've borrowed a Sundance truck."

On his way to the front door he noticed his father smoothing back his hair, and Matt smiled. Wallace was sober and worried about his appearance. Good sign.

"I was getting antsy, and Trace told me to use his truck," Nikki said as she entered the house. "I left a message on your phone that I was coming. Is he sober?"

His phone was upstairs. Still, no harm, no foul. "Fine. Having coffee in the kitchen." He motioned for her to go first but she shook her head and shoved him in front of her.

Wallace was sitting at the table, looking small and harmless. He offered a tentative smile, his worried eyes following Nikki. "Would you like coffee?" he asked, and started to rise.

"I'll get it." With a glance at the table, Matt motioned for Nikki to sit. "You want one?" he asked her. "Fresh Columbian."

"No, thanks." She took a seat, her skittering gaze landing everywhere but on the man sitting across from her.

Matt started to break the ice, then decided to let his father do it. Until the damn silence seemed to last longer than an eight-second ride on a pissed-off bull.

Then Wallace said two words Matt never in his life thought he'd hear him say. "I'm sorry." Wallace noisily cleared his throat, but his voice still wobbled when he continued. "For abandoning you and your mother. It's important to me that you know I loved Rosa, and I wanted to be with her. But I already had a wife and son, and I had to protect them."

Matt stared at the years of guilt and shame etched in his father's ravaged face. In some perverted way, he had sacrificed for Matt and his mother. He'd been wrong to have the affair in the first place. So much of what his father had done in his life had been wrong, as a parent and a husband, but seeing him in this new light did something funny inside of Matt.

He glanced at Nikki, her expression blank. She always fought hard to control her emotions, but he knew it hurt her to hear this. She'd deserved her father's loyalty and support as much as Matt. She took a deep breath and her features relaxed, a little sad but not angry. Hell, the man was dying and she probably felt like Matt did…what was the point?

"I resented you for a long time," Nikki said softly. "At first I didn't understand why you couldn't love me, then I was angry because I saw how much you'd hurt Mom. But you know what?" She started to reach for Wallace's shriveled hand but then pulled back and folded hers on the table. "Mom and I are really close. We had each other, and I never doubted for a single day that she loved me with all her heart."

Wallace smiled a little. "That's Rosa. She doted on you."

"Were you jealous?" Nikki asked, her eyes pools of fresh hurt. "Is that why you stopped coming?" She made a small sound of distress. "No, don't answer. It doesn't matter." After a sharp intake of breath, she rushed on. "I'm glad you sent her money. Thank you for that. She worked hard to make ends meet, but what you sent really helped and it gave us more time together."

Matt grabbed the coffeepot, sweat already popping out on the back of his neck. "Refill?" he asked his father, who shook his head and covered his mug with a trembling hand.

His gaze briefly slid away from Nikki. "What I did was wrong," he said, his voice choked with shame. "I was furious with Rosa for refusing to see me because I hadn't legally acknowledged you. But I had no call to stop the checks after two years."

"What? But you didn't." Nikki frowned, glanced over at Matt.

His heart hammering in his chest, he shrugged. "Dad, you should lie down for a while. You don't look so hot."

"Mom was the one who stopped you from sending the money orders," Nikki said. "After I quit community college." Looking confused, Nikki and Wallace stared at each other. "That was a year ago."

Wallace squinted as if trying to remember. "It wasn't me," he murmured, his expression a swirl of panic and confusion like a man who thought he was losing his mind.

Matt sighed. "It was Mom. She started sending money a year after you stopped. After she died, I took over." He could barely bring himself to look at Nikki.

Her eyes turned black with emotion, going from stunned to hurt to furious in seconds. "You lied to me?

"Technically, no."

"Screw you, Matt." She got to her feet. "Screw both of you."

"Catherine knew about Rosa?" Wallace clutched the table.

"Nikki, wait." Matt started to go after her, but she was running for the front door and he knew she'd reach the truck before he could stop her. He wouldn't chase her and risk her wrapping herself around a telephone pole.

He watched from the window as she sped down the driveway, knowing the look she'd given him would haunt him forever. As if she thought that by hiding the truth, Matt had treated her no better than Wallace had.

18

WALLACE STAYED IN the chair, his shoulders drooping, his blank stare aimed at the empty doorway. Damn, he looked shaky and a lot like a man who needed a drink. What did it matter now? Nikki wasn't likely to return, or have anything to say to either of them…except maybe go to hell.

"I'll go talk to her." Matt set his mug in the sink. "Stay here. I won't be long," he said, but Wallace just kept staring, showing no sign he'd heard. "Dad?"

He looked up then and nodded.

Matt ran upstairs for his phone and keys. Before leaving he checked in again on Wallace. He hadn't moved.

Since the truck was borrowed, he assumed Nikki was headed for the Sundance. That would be his first stop. He had to try and explain the promise he'd made his mother. She'd wanted Nikki and Rosa to believe the money had come from Wallace. No use the girl growing up completely bitter, she'd said.

Rachel was waiting on the porch for him when he arrived. Nikki had beat him by five minutes and was in her room. "I think she was crying," Rachel said. "What happened?"

"The money. It came up before I could tell her and now she's pissed at Wallace and me." He pushed a hand through his hair, avoiding Rachel's eyes. "I need to talk to her."

"She's probably more hurt than angry. Give her some time to calm down." Rachel turned when the front door opened, and smiled at the three women who came outside.

Matt nodded at them, but made it real clear he wasn't in the mood to visit by staring off toward the mountains as they passed.

Behind him he heard Trace's voice coming from the direction of the stables. Then he caught a glimpse of Cole near the barn. Great. The whole family was around today. "Your mom inside?"

"In the kitchen," Rachel said with a sympathetic look, then took his arm. "Let's go for a walk."

He wouldn't budge. "I know you mean well, but I have to—"

"She doesn't want to talk to you right now." Rachel let out a sigh of frustration. "I'm sorry. She asked me to tell you."

Jesus, first he'd put her in the middle, and now Nikki had. He let Rachel steer him around the south side of the house, neither of them speaking as they avoided patches of snow. The ground was still soggy, and his boots were taking a beating, but he kept walking.

"Did she say anything else?" he asked finally.

"No, just that she thought you might follow her."

"I'm sorry." He shoved his cold hands into his pockets. "I know you have work to do."

"It's okay." She hugged his arm. "It's nice to walk."

"Right, in thirty-degree weather."

"You big wuss, we can turn around if you want."

Matt smiled. "I saw Cole and Trace. Is Jesse around? I want to tell them about finding the trailer."

She stopped and stared up at him, shading her eyes. They were so green in the sunlight. "Did you talk to Wallace?"

"I did." He had to look away. "He didn't know anything about it. I told him it was probably Tony and Eddie."

"Then you'll have to call Noah as soon as possible so he can locate them. I believe he'll be back in the office today."

"I'm gonna make sure everyone gets their stuff back. I don't know that it's worth pursuing."

"I hope it's that simple," Rachel said quietly. "Your father has made a lot of enemies, and since the items were found on his property... Matt, people are going to be angry."

He saw it in her eyes, the pity and concern, saw the way she studied his face. She knew that he didn't believe his father was blameless. He'd never been able to hide anything from her. He wasn't even sure why he was trying.

They walked in silence for another ten mintues, then Matt stopped. "Let's go back while your brothers are still around. I wanna get this over with." He lifted a loose curl off her shoulder and twirled it around his finger. "You just found out about it."

"Yes, if you don't mind, that would be best." She slid an arm around his waist, even though he didn't deserve her, not even a little.

They walked back to the house, motioning for Trace, who was working with a black stallion in the corral. Cole was nowhere in sight, but Rachel somehow communicated they wanted him because Trace stopped in the barn, and then both men walked toward the porch where he and Rachel waited.

"We'll get my mom and go to Cole's office," she said, lowering her arm from around his waist. Then she squinted past his shoulder. "Might be Jesse. But he doesn't drive that fast."

Matt turned and saw dust plumes. The vehicle had to be moving at a hell of a clip to kick up that much dry dirt under the gravel. The air fled Matt's lungs. It was Wallace's SUV that came barreling and swerving toward the house.

Skipping the steps, Matt jumped off the porch and charged toward the vehicle. He heard Rachel scream his name but he kept moving, his pulse racing out of control. The SUV stopped not three feet in front of him. Through the windshield he saw

Wallace's flushed face, and knew the bastard was drunk even before he staggered out.

"What the hell are you doing here?" Matt grabbed his shirt before he fell backward. "I told you to stay put."

"You don't tell me shit, boy." Spit flew from Wallace's mouth. Rage filled his eyes as he leaned to his left and glared past Matt. "Yeah, I took your damn horse trailer, and I'm not sorry. You goddamn McAllisters think you're better than everyone." He turned his head and spit in the gravel.

Matt knew Cole and Trace were behind him and he was tempted to release Wallace, let his ass land on the cold hard ground. "Not everyone." Matt fisted the shirt tighter. "Just better than you. And they're right."

"What's he talking about?" Cole's pinched voice came from just over Matt's shoulder. "Where's our trailer?"

Maintaining his hold, Matt turned to face him.

"It's safe and in good shape, Cole," Rachel said, rushing toward them, Trace alongside her. "Matt was about to explain."

Trace and Cole both stared at their sister. "You knew?" Trace said, his puzzled frown slowly sliding to anger.

Cole's eyes blazed, boring into her, demanding the truth.

"She just found out," Matt said. "I just told her."

A guilty blush burned in her cheeks. She opened her mouth but couldn't seem to speak, only swallowed convulsively.

Matt stared in horror. She was going to confess. "Rachel."

She wouldn't look at him. "Yesterday. I knew yesterday." Her voice caught and she hung her head.

"No." Matt turned his back on Wallace to face the brothers. They were pissed, and rightfully so. "She's confused."

"What's going on out here?" Barbara stood on the porch, slowly stepping down, her startled gaze riveted on Wallace.

"Mom, go inside, please," Cole said, but she ignored him.

Matt felt his father lurch against him. His whole body shook, and Matt caught him by the elbow.

"Barbara." Even his voice quaked. "Why didn't you come to me after Catherine was gone? We were both free. You knew I still loved you. You knew," he murmured, sagging heavily on Matt, his voice dropping. "You and Rosa, the only two women I ever loved."

Matt jerked away. "What did you say?"

Wallace slid to the bumper, his eyes wary, apparently not drunk enough to disregard the anger he'd stoked in Matt.

"Did you ever love my mother?" Matt glared, his hands fisting. Had he been talking about Barbara the other day? What the hell…

In spite of himself, he glanced at Rachel, then her brothers, their anger tempered with bafflement. When he dared to look at Barbara, he saw no confusion whatsoever.

"I saw you," Wallace said, his eyes getting mean. "Don't think I don't know you've been sneaking around with Jeb Collins."

Barbara swept a look of panic at her children. "Stop it, Wallace. You're making a fool of yourself."

His weak gravelly laugh dislodged the spittle caking the corners of his mouth. "You should've come to me instead of whoring yourself out."

Cole and Trace lunged at him, but Rachel and Barbara each grabbed an arm. They clung to them, yelling and begging for them to back off.

Matt already had a firm grip on the bastard. It was his temper he was having trouble holding on to. Fury burned so hot in his gut he knew he had to get him to town. Get Wallace locked up before Matt did something he'd regret for the rest of his life.

"I'm taking him to Noah," he said, barely able to meet anyone's eyes as he dragged the old man to the truck.

He shoved him into the passenger side, and when he came around the hood he saw Rachel rushing toward him. Her brothers stood near their mother, watching Rachel with resentment. Matt had done that to her, to all of them.

He yanked open the driver's door, but he couldn't climb in before she got to him. "I'm sorry, Rachel," he said quietly. "So damn sorry." He jerked away when she tried to clutch his arm. "Go back to your family. They love you. It'll be okay."

"Don't do anything hasty. Please. Noah won't be back until later. Let everyone cool off. Including you." Her heart was in her eyes, and it was breaking in half in front of him.

He didn't say anything. He couldn't speak. So he got in the truck, started the engine and drove off without looking back.

RACHEL STARED AFTER MATT until the truck disappeared, but the devastation on his face stayed imprinted in her memory. Every instinct screamed at her to go after him. Once he left Blackfoot Falls, she'd never see him again. It would be over between them. Just like that. Just as quickly as their relationship had reignited.

Pressing a hand to the churning in her belly, she turned back to the house. Her mother and brothers hadn't moved. They watched her, the disappointment on Cole's and Trace's face clear even from twenty yards away. Her brothers would never forgive her. She wasn't sure she could forgive herself.

Her mom sighed. "Let's all go into the house. It seems I have some explaining to do." She waited for Rachel, then put an arm around her shoulders, hugging her as they walked to the porch.

Cole and Trace followed, saying nothing until they'd settled in the den. Then Cole said, "My office would be more private."

"Hilda, Jamie and Nikki are upstairs. No one else is here. I wish Jesse was. He needs to hear this, too." She sounded calm, but Rachel knew her mom was nervous when she huddled deep in the brown leather chair and curled her legs under her. "Clearly Wallace and I have a history. He's five years older than me and when I was a senior in high school he asked me to marry him." She sighed when Trace muttered a mild curse.

"The proposal came out of the blue. I knew he had a crush on me but we hadn't dated. There'd been a dance at the town festival, and he'd bought me a soda. But I was already getting serious about your father. Catherine Gunderson—she was Weaver then—was a friend of mine and I knew she was sweet on Wallace. I made it clear I wasn't interested but he persisted.

"Then I married your father a year after I graduated, and Wallace and Catherine started going together. My friendship with her was a bit rocky at times, but we stayed in touch and our relationship actually strengthened later in life. She was lonely. God knows she loved Wallace till the end, but it wasn't easy being married to him."

"How come we didn't know?" Rachel asked. "I mean, when did you ever see Mrs. Gunderson?"

"I'd visit her when Wallace was away or we'd talk on the phone. Sometimes she'd come by when you kids were in school. Obviously your father knew the story about Wallace. So when Wallace started drinking and baiting him, your father understood it was never about the land. In his own warped way, Wallace was trying to prove he was a better man than your dad. He wanted to own something that belonged to Gavin McAllister. It's sad, and I always felt bad for Catherine. And Matt." She looked at Rachel. "I sent the letter about his father being ill. I'd promised Catherine to keep in touch with Matt and help however I could."

"I can't believe you never said a word to us." Trace sat hunched forward, his elbows resting on his thighs. "All these years the guy has been a—" He tightened his mouth. "You could've said something."

"What good would it have done?" Barbara pulled the afghan from over the chair onto her lap. "Look, the past is irrelevant, and, by the way, my business," she said sternly, and

Trace frowned. "But I'm sorry I didn't tell you that I've been seeing someone for about eight months now. For that I owe you an apology. I have no excuse except that I didn't know how you'd react. But Jeb Collins is a very nice man, and you'll meet him soon. He owns a ranch in Norton County. Cole, I think you know him."

Cole nodded, a grudging smile pulling at his mouth. "He's outbid us at a couple of auctions."

Rachel noticed how her mom's eyes had lit up when she'd mentioned Jeb's name. Even her cheeks had turned a bit pink. It was great to see the life in her face. Rachel would've appreciated it more if her shame wasn't threatening to drown her.

"I have an apology to make, too," she said, her voice wobbly. "I am so, so sorry I didn't tell you about the trailer. I only found out yesterday, and Matt asked me if we could keep it between us, just overnight, until he found out who was responsible—"

"You still could've told us," Trace said, his expression more hurt than angry. "Didn't mean we had to act on it."

Rachel swallowed. "Of course, you're right. But I—"

"I completely disagree."

They all turned to their mother and her no-nonsense tone.

"A day wouldn't make a difference, but your relationship with Matt was at stake, Rachel. Matt needed to know he could count on you and that you believed in him." Barbara met each of her children's eyes. "You had a wonderful father, who lived for this family. We did our best to be accessible and loving parents. To give you the guidance you needed without smothering you.

"Matt didn't grow up in that kind of environment. As much as I liked Catherine, I hated how her blindness to Wallace's behavior interfered with her being a mother to Matt. The poor boy had no parental support and the abuse he took…." She shook her head. "Nevertheless, he seems to have made himself into a fine and honorable young man."

Trace sat up straight, eyes riveted to the empty doorway. He started to get up when Nikki stepped into view.

"I'm sorry," she said. "I didn't mean to eavesdrop. I was just coming down the stairs and I heard—" Her voice broke, her dark eyes glassy from unshed tears. "You're right, Barbara, and I was so mean to him. He's always trying so hard to help." She sniffed. "At least I had my mother, but Matt had no one."

"Well, I wouldn't say no one." Barbara smiled. "He had Rachel," she said, and Rachel coughed. "Yes, I knew you used to sneak off to see him. And now he has you, too, Nikki. Come sit with us."

Trace immediately made room for her next to him, but Nikki shook her head. "Thanks, but I didn't mean to intrude. Though I'm glad I overheard because—" She gave them a small smile and moved back, clearing her throat. "I need to call my brother."

Rachel didn't try to stop her. She understood because she wanted to call him, too. No, not just call, she wanted to see him. Touch him. Hold him in her arms. But she still hadn't absolved herself.

Once Nikki was gone, Rachel faced her mom. "Nothing happened, you know...when I used to sneak off with Matt." Rachel's cheeks heated up, and for the life of her she didn't know why she'd offered the information. Trace's snort didn't help. "Matt said I was too young," she murmured. "I wanted you to know."

"I can't say that I didn't worry a time or two, especially with you reeling from Dad's death. But I trusted that you'd both be sensible." She stared at Rachel for a long moment. "When I saw that you two were hitting it off again, I admit I was nervous because I didn't know Matt anymore. We'd only exchanged a few letters. But I think he's a good man."

"For what it's worth, I agree." Cole sighed. "Initially I was pissed about the trailer, but I don't blame you for keeping his confidence. You did the right thing." He got to his feet. "I'm just not sure how this is going to play out."

"Wallace is dying, Cole. I doubt I have to keep that a secret at this point," Rachel said. "We can press charges and have him locked up but it doesn't make sense."

He nodded, glanced at Trace and their mother. "We'll see what we can do. In the meantime, I've got men waiting on me in the barn."

Rachel watched her brothers leave, then found it wasn't easy to look at her mother. Maybe that was a sign to keep her mouth shut because she was feeling too emotional to sensor herself.

"I have something else to confess." Rachel braced herself, then blurted, "I hadn't planned on staying in Blackfoot Falls past the summer."

Her mother seemed concerned but not surprised. "I hope you didn't already have something lined up that you turned down."

"Not exactly. I— Wait. You expected me to leave?"

"You're bright and ambitious. Why wouldn't you want to see what's out there?"

"I've felt so guilty."

"Oh, honey." Her mother left the chair to sit beside Rachel on the couch. "Guilt should rest on my shoulders, not yours. The dude ranch idea was a godsend, but I wouldn't have had a clue where to start. I guessed it might be holding you back but I didn't want to see your brothers struggling so hard to keep the Sundance afloat. I told myself you still had time to pursue a career. I was thrilled when Jamie said she was moving here. For Cole's sake, of course, but I knew she'd be company for you, too. I heard she offered you a chance to travel."

Rachel nodded without enthusiasm. She had to give Jamie an answer soon. The idea no longer appealed.

"I have a question…what was your first thought today when I admitted I was seeing someone?"

Rachel shrugged. "That it's great." She smiled. "It's about time. And I wish you would've told us sooner."

"Then what?"

At a loss, she shrugged again. "That's it."

"So you didn't think, yay, mom has someone and now I don't have to feel bad about leaving her?"

Rachel stared at her mother. A couple weeks ago that was exactly what she would've thought.

Laughing, she patted Rachel's leg and got to her feet. "I have a feeling you're not so anxious to leave anymore. Now, go talk to Matt, before he does something foolish."

AT THE LAST MOMENT, Matt turned toward the Lone Wolf instead of heading to town. He still had every intention of turning the bastard in, but he was too angry to drive, too angry to trust himself to make any kind of reasonable decision.

He glanced over at Wallace, slumped in the seat, chin to his chest and snoring. Jesus, how much havoc he'd caused and now he was sleeping like a friggin' baby. Matt gripped the wheel more firmly, rattled that minutes ago he'd been barely able to control the violence inside him. He didn't want to be the young hothead he'd been in the beginning of his career. That guy who'd taken too many risks, who hadn't cared if he walked out of the ring or not.

Though he wasn't sure why it mattered. He was a Gunderson. No one in Blackfoot Falls expected more from him. As far as Rachel went, he'd been fooling himself if he thought they were headed anywhere. He'd been right all along. He was a weak, foolish man who hadn't grown up. How could he have hurt the woman he loved? And for Wallace?

Matt swerved to miss a rabbit hopping across the driveway. Maybe he'd made another mistake by not taking Wallace straight to town. No, as pissed as he was, he knew he'd end up fixing things with Noah and the victims, see to it that Wallace remained at home. If only in honor of his mother's memory. She wouldn't want to see the old man dying in a jail cell.

When he got to the house he pulled as close to the door as he could, then helped Wallace inside. Instead of tackling the stairs, Matt left him stretched out on his office couch. A half bottle of whiskey was on the table, and Matt started to move it but stopped himself. He was done playing the parent, the caretaker, the go-between for Wallace, Nikki, anyone.

No good had come of his actions so far, and now he'd blown it with Rachel. The thought tore at him, even knowing it was just a fling for her. She'd said as much….

She'd also said she'd once dreamed of marrying him. The idea alone pressed all his pleasure buttons. Made his heart turn over and his pulse race like the devil. He went to the window and stared out at the big blue sky. Did she mean it that he made it hard for her to leave? Rachel had never been the type to tease when it came down to the serious stuff. Even as a kid she'd been plainspoken.

"Shit." Matt rubbed his gritty eyes, then turned to look at Wallace. He'd always been pathetic, and he'd end up dying a pathetic man. And dammit, Matt wasn't him. He was nothing like his father. Rachel wouldn't love someone like that.

The thought struck from out of the blue. She'd never said she loved him, not outright. But her eyes and smile and touch had told him many times. If he'd only given her the chance, she might've whispered the words….

Hell, he knew he loved her and he hadn't told her either.

No, he wasn't as smart as her, but he had a lot going for him at this stage of his career—the money, celebrity…. He'd turn his back on all of it in a heartbeat for a simple life with Rachel. Why couldn't he believe she'd want the same? Talk about getting the raw end of the deal. How could he compete with all the dreams she'd already shoved aside for her family? She deserved to travel the world, to seek her own adventures.

Still, he knew what he had to do. Tell her the truth and let her make her own choice. If this trip had taught him one thing, it was that keeping secrets was a fool's game. It never worked out for anyone.

He headed back out to his truck. It wouldn't be easy returning to the Sundance. The McAllisters had to hate his guts. And if the brothers wanted to beat the crap out of him, so be it. Seeing Rachel, telling her how he felt was all that mattered. It hurt like hell to think she might turn him away, but he'd let the chips fall where they may. No way would he be the guy who left without a word again.

RACHEL CLIMBED INTO her mother's car and took a deep breath while inserting the key. She had the time it took to drive to the Lone Wolf to rehearse what she wanted to say. Though she'd probably forget every word the moment she laid eyes on him. She started to reverse but stopped the car when she saw his truck.

Her heart fluttering like crazy, she turned off the engine and got out of the car as he pulled in beside her. She hadn't been this nervous, not ever in her life. So much hung in the balance. It was entirely possible that Matt was here to say goodbye. So she'd have to be quick and brave because she wasn't going to let him go without telling him how she felt.

They stood in the chilly air as Matt stared into her eyes. "You were on your way out. I'll only keep you a minute."

"I was going to see you."

Hope lit up his face and squeezed her heart. "I'm sorry, Rachel, for getting between you and your family. Hell, I'm sorry for being a Gunderson but—"

"Stop. Quit buying into that Gunderson name crap. You're your own man, a really terrific man and I wish you could see it as clearly as I do. So just stop. I mean it."

Matt smiled. "You sure? Because I was just getting to the good part."

She lifted a hand, shading her eyes so she could better see his face. He took her shoulders and moved her out of the sun's glare, then surprised her by looping his arms around her waist.

"Tell me," she said impatiently. "What were you going to say?"

He pulled her closer. "I love you, Rachel McAllister," he said, his eyes so blue and earnest. "I think I always have."

The world tilted on its axis as the words she'd longed to hear since she was a girl sank in. "Oh, Matt." She was not going to cry. God, not now. "I love you, too. So much sometimes I feel like I'm going to explode."

He shuddered on a deep exhale. "I don't have it all worked out yet, but I'm pretty sure I'm going to stay on, talk to Nikki about us taking over the Lone Wolf together. That is, if you'd even want to stay in Blackfoot Falls. I don't want to steal any of your dreams, Rachel. If you want to go off on adventures and see the world, that's fine. I'll wait. If you want me to. I'd wait a lifetime if that's what it takes."

The tears she'd blinked away came back with a vengeance. She knew he was telling her the truth. He'd struggled so hard to come home, and even though he had to deal with all the complications of being with his father, she was proud of him for wanting to make the Lone Wolf his home. Proud of him for so much.

"You know, my family spent a small fortune on my education," she said, "but all I've ever wanted was to find my place in the world. Everything changed the day you rode back into town. Now when I think about my place, it's with you. And maybe a couple babies. Someday."

"You mean that?"

She nodded. "I was so afraid you were coming to tell me goodbye."

Matt wiped a tear from her cheek. "Not gonna happen again. Ever. I'm a bull rider," he said. "I know how to hang on tight and never let go."

"You'd better, Matt Gunderson. Because I've loved you for a long time, and I will hold you to that."

"You have my word, darlin'. I'm not going anywhere."

When he kissed her, the world tilted again, right to where it was supposed to be.

* * * * *

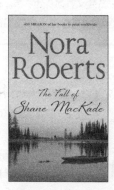